MORE STORIES TO MAKE YOU BLUSH

Marie Gray

More Stories to Make You Blush

Seven Naughty Tales

Translated by Emma Stark

 **Green Frog Publishing**

Canadian Cataloguing in Publication Data

Gray, Marie, 1963-
More Stories to make you blush
Translation of: Nouvelles histoires à faire rougir.

ISBN 2-89455-096-0

© Guy Saint-Jean Éditeur Inc. 2001

Translation: Emma Stark
Cover illustration: Lucie Crovatto
Graphic Design: Christiane Séguin

Legal Deposit first quarter 2001
Bibliothèque nationale du Québec and The National Library of Canada
ISBN 2-89455-096-0

The Publisher gratefully acknowledges the assistance of the Province of Québec,
through the SODEC (Société de développement des entreprises culturelles) and
the support of the Government of Canada, through the Book Publishing Industry
Development Program.

Green Frog Publishing is an imprint of Guy Saint-Jean Éditeur
3172, boul. Industriel, Laval (Québec) Canada H7L 4P7. Tel.: (450) 663-1777.
Fax.: (450) 663-6666.

Printed in the United States of America

Caught in the Act

$\mathscr{I}$remember that morning very well, Wednesday, October 12. Now, there was a morning I should have never gotten out of bed! When the alarm clock rang, pulling me out of a deep slumber, my wife was still sound asleep, her flannel nightgown buttoned up to the neck, her face smothered in "rejuvenating" night cream. I vaguely recall that I'd been having a dream before the alarm went off with its godawful racket. I dreamed that my tender spouse, divested of both nightgown and cream, had slid under the sheets and was heartily sucking me, something she hadn't been inclined to do for many long years. I love her dearly, but at this stage of the game, our relations are more and more platonic...

But back to the morning of October 12. I'd had a bad cold for about a week. The day looked pretty gray, though at that hour it was too dark to tell for sure. A little voice in my head kept urging, "Stay in bed! Treat yourself, just this once!... when've you ever been sick?" I was sorely tempted. It's true, I'd never taken advantage of my "sick days". I thought of how wonderful it would be to shut off the damn clock and sleep all morning in the warmth of the conjugal bed. But duty called. I like my work. I'm a security guard for the Fashion Gallery department store, and after many long years of service I spend my days comfortably seated, watching monitors that display whatever's happening in different parts of the establishment.

But I didn't get the job — a job made in heaven! — because of my pretty face. I could spend the whole day sitting without having to do rounds of the departments. I didn't have to carry a weapon — I hate firearms! — because I was out of harm's way. Not that much ever happened. I had only witnessed two armed robberies in my entire career. Not bad, for almost forty years of service. Still, I far prefer the security of my job, especially at my age. I don't want to be chasing petty thieves or loitering teenagers. And let's be frank: why would I spend the day standing when I could be sitting?

When Management for the Fashion Gallery installed the new security system, they had a hell of a time deciding who to trust with the job of supervising it all. It wasn't that there were so many cameras — eighteen isn't a lot. The delicate matter was the cameras in the fitting rooms. A lot of security agents volunteered for the job, hoping to spend the day watching women undress. But they just didn't understand! I am extremely proud of the work I do. And if Management trusted me with the job, it's because I'm a professional and won't spend more time than necessary watching those booths. It's not that I'm stupid, but I figure if a woman can't do her shopping without having to wonder who might be watching while she's trying on clothes, it's really a shame! So they also had to find someone who would keep his mouth shut. The Fashion Gallery had no intention of letting people know that they followed their woman customers right into the fitting rooms! That would've been a disaster. All sorts of organizations would've stuck their noses in, and that would've been it, no more cameras in the fitting rooms. And yet, it's right in these little booths that most shoplifting occurs.

In any case, it was me who got the job, thanks to my experience, discretion and professionalism. And I've caught more than one woman shoplifting! Sure, it'd be tempting to sit and watch the fitting rooms all day... the ladies who shop at the Fashion Gallery are usually fairly well off, beautiful and elegant. But I'm too old for that kind of nonsense, and I secretly hope our competitors choose their employees with care when it comes to handing out this kind of task.

Anyway, that morning it was the call of duty that gave me the courage to resist the coaxing of my inner voice. With great difficulty I hauled myself out of bed, casting an envious glance at my better half, still sleeping, and headed for the shower. I thought I'd forgotten my dream, but the memory suddenly returned at the sight of my erect member under the spray of hot water. I imagined the mouth of my sweet Margaret gently taking it prisoner, and licking it with appetite like she used to do, back in the days when she slept naked and without face cream... Absentmindedly I soaped my cock, sliding my hand up and down, feeling my heart beat faster. When was the last time I'd stroked that lazy rod? I was pleasantly surprised by my state of desire and thought of waking Margaret to share it with her. But the moment passed, and I figured she wouldn't be quite as receptive as my hard and swollen member. I came with a shudder, hurried to clean myself up, and went to work.

The morning was slow. Not a single thing happened to break the tedium — that is, not until She made her entrance, the one who would wake my groggy instincts with a jolt and turn my life upside down.

I first saw her on the monitor for the main entrance. She was around twenty-five, blonde, classy and beautifully groomed. I see pretty women come through those doors every day, but this one was enough to knock the wind out of you. She seemed in a hurry, like a lot of customers who come looking for a specific item over their lunch break. She headed straight for the lingerie section. I watched her body, her every move. She moved gracefully despite her elegant high-heeled shoes and form-fitting suit. Her hair was perfect, not a strand out of place, and I was sure she was wearing one of those alluring and very expensive perfumes like Shalimar or Opium. At the women's lingerie section, she removed her gloves with a slow and deliberate gesture that gave me a hard on for some inexplicable reason. She looked so sure of herself! Probably the difficult type who demands top quality and flawless service. Luckily the young salesgirl knew her stuff. She suggested a few different styles and showed her to the fitting rooms. I took a deep breath. It was the chance of a lifetime, but I told myself there was no way I was going to take advantage of it... Except it would've taken superhuman strength to resist. I was at a loss to understand why I felt this sudden, irresistible attraction to a woman I didn't know. I'm usually so respectful of our women customers' privacy, but I was totally unable, in body and mind, to take my eyes off the fitting room monitors. Instead, I tried desperately to guess which one she'd be given. The clerk led her to number 3. The beautiful stranger went in. I gave myself a one-minute time limit, barely enough even to get a clear view of her; after that, I told myself, I would go back to my responsibilities...

Before I go on, I should explain that I've always been faithful to my wife, in thought, word and deed. Last month we celebrated our thirty-fifth wedding anniversary. I was moved, happy, proud, and considered myself lucky to have spent so many years by her side in quiet happiness, free of dramas, and I hoped to spend the rest of my life that way. I'm still hoping! I may be moved by the sight of a pretty young woman wearing a skirt that's too short, but that doesn't mean I don't love my wife... even if I sometimes try and guess what's underneath that skirt. These things happen! I think Margaret still loves me too. If not, she wouldn't be so sweet and considerate with me. Our children left home years ago, and my wife and I still enjoy each other's company. The quiet evenings we spend watching TV with a couple of beers prove how comfortable we are together. It's modest but it's cosy. Still, it's been awhile since Margaret stopped watching her weight or wearing flattering clothes like the woman in the store...

The cameras in the fitting rooms are behind the mirrors. I could see her gorgeous face more clearly now. Her careful makeup brought out her pale eyes whose colour, unfortunately, I couldn't see. All you can see on these blasted screens is umpteen shades of gray! But no matter, she was a striking beauty. She hung up her purse on one of the hooks and with her long fingers unbuttoned her suit jacket. I told myself that was enough: I wouldn't watch her take off her blouse, skirt and the rest. But under the jacket she wore nothing but a bra. A cleverly folded scarf had created the illusion of a blouse. I'd been caught at my own game! It was too late to tear my eyes away. I was mesmerized. Her magnificent brassiere was made of lace, and as she unhooked her skirt, I saw she was wearing matching panties. The skirt slid to the floor and she slowly picked it up, hanging it up carefully so it wouldn't get wrinkled. Why did she have to be wearing those stockings that miraculously stay up on the thighs? They were very pale and silky, enveloping her willowy legs and resting on her white skin. With precise gestures, she took off the bra, then slipped off the panties before removing the new lingerie from the hangers. It crossed my mind that she shouldn't be taking her panties off, they ask the customers to leave them on when trying clothes, but this thought vanished from my mind as quickly as it had arrived. She had a splendid body: big firm breasts, a narrow waist, rounded hips, flat stomach... I knew she was a real blonde from the pale bush between her legs. She turned, and I admired the roundness of her buttocks, the slender and elegant back, the slim arms hooking up the new brassiere, sliding the panties up her luscious legs. The lingerie set suited her to perfection, the salesgirl had given her admirable advice. The lace was so delicate you could see her nipples and the little shadow over her sex. She examined herself with a serious look, turning to study her body from different angles, obviously asking herself if the items were really what she wanted. After a few moments, her face lit up with an angelic smile. She liked what she saw, her mind was made up. I was hoping she would try the other bra-and-panty sets that she had brought in, but she didn't. She was satisfied on the very first try. She started to get dressed, taking off the new lingerie, allowing me to admire that fabulous body in its nudity before covering it up again with chic clothes. She went out and paid for her purchase, a little smile of satisfaction on her face as she waited for her package. The smile stayed on her face as she went through the store. I gave a nervous little jump when, just before going through the door, she turned, looked back, then raised her head to the camera over the entrance. I blushed like a teenager who's been caught red-handed. I had the strange feeling she knew I was there, that she guessed I had been watching her greedily and found her beautiful. So beautiful that when I got up from my station, there was an obvious bulge in the lap of my pants, like the centre pole of a tent, pointing straight up and hard.

* * *

That evening when I got home, I could only mumble a vague reply when Margaret greeted me with her eternal: "Paul, is that you? Did you have a good day?" I hurried into the bedroom to take off my clothes, and jumped in the shower to cool down my fevered thoughts. She found it strange that I was taking another shower, but I explained that there'd been trouble with the air-conditioning and it had been hellishly hot all day. I was filled with a horrible feeling of guilt telling her this lie. I also went over and kissed her. I was as surprised as she was by the tenderness and depth of that kiss. She stepped back, turning red with confusion, and fixed me with her most piercing gaze, the one you couldn't hide anything from.

— What's going on with you? Come on, out with it!

I took a deep breath.

— Well, actually, I was thinking of you all day. I know I'm not good at showing it, but... I love you. It's been a long time since I've told you... that's all.

She laughed and gave me a big hug.

She made me an excellent meal and as I watched her bustle around the kitchen, I felt another surprise erection coming on. I felt awkward as a schoolboy, though we'd been married so long! But it had been years since our passion had cooled, and I don't think either of us knew how to break the little layer of ice that had grown between us. Should I show her right away how she had affected me? Or be more subtle and try to get her to come to bed early? I couldn't make up my mind and asked myself so many questions that my erection drooped back down to where it came from. In the end, it was a night like any other, with us sitting in our separate chairs, watching TV.

* * *

The next day, Thursday, October 13, She made another appearance, the woman I'd already started to call "my" customer. Same time of day, same hurried look. She went straight to the lingerie section and picked out one of the bra-and-panty sets she hadn't tried the day before. I didn't even attempt to turn away this time. The same old guilt shyly raised its head, but it was far from stopping me. This time I made myself right at home in front of the screens for fitting room 6, and watched the beautiful stranger. She started with the same routine as the day before, this time wearing a dress with buttons that she undid one by one to free her divine body. That day she was wearing a pretty black camisole that looked like it was made of silk, and adorable stockings, black as well. Her body began to move to the rhythm of music I couldn't hear. I watched this lustful little dance, mesmerized by her fluid movements. She ran her fingers through her hair, then trailed them down to her shoulders in an intimate embrace. She fondled her full, luscious breasts through the silky fabric and I could see her nipples grow erect, begging for a caress. But instead of her breasts it was her thighs her hands were caressing, gently massaging the velvety white flesh. She kept on dancing, bending down and spreading her legs. I saw then that her sex was covered only by the barest wisp of lace to which her fingers were moving dangerously close, as if answering some irresistible call. All at once she straightened up, as if realizing what a strange situation she was in. She looked around confused, like someone waking from a dream. She hurriedly pulled on the lingerie she'd brought in with her, but seemed disappointed by the way it looked. She quickly got dressed again, left the fitting room and handed the bra and panties to Nicole, the salesgirl. She hurried out of the store, leaving me panting at the edge of my chair, feeling let down and far too excited for my own good.

That night I mumbled the same excuse to Margaret, then escaped into the shower and jerked off with wild abandon. What was happening to me? Why did that woman have such a hold over me? I'd masturbated more in the past two days than in the last twelve years put together!

* * *

Friday, October 14, I went to the job preparing myself mentally for "my" customer's visit. It didn't seem likely that she'd come three days in a row, but after the previous day's display, I could only hope she would return to satisfy my horny curiosity. I tried to muster the strength to resist, in case she did come back. But I knew it was a lost cause. I'd dreamt of her the night before and woke up feeling sheepish, looking over at my dear Margaret, sound asleep and unsuspecting. I felt like a liar and a louse, as if I'd cheated on her. I was mad at myself, but at the same time tried to convince myself that I hadn't done anything wrong. And in reality, I hadn't... it was just my mind and body that had behaved like a couple of jerks.

When I saw her come in at the usual time, I desperately tried steering my eyes towards the other screens. In a few fractions of a second, I saw her select a pale negligee. Not long after, Nicole guided her to the fitting rooms. That was all it took. Again my eyes were glued to the screen, and all my good intentions were gone with the wind.

She was completely undressed except for her stockings and shoes, but instead of putting on the negligee she grabbed her thick hair and piled it carelessly on top of her head. She took a look at herself, again pivoting to get a better look, then let her hands slide down her neck to her breasts, lightly stroking her erect nipples. She leaned forward and picked up the silky camisole that I suppose she'd been wearing before — was it beige or pink? I could only imagine its wonderful, subtle harmony with the colour of her skin. She rubbed it over her generous breasts then wrapped it around her waist, letting the delicate fabric tickle her round buttocks.

Suddenly she seized one end of the camisole, and slid the other between her legs. Before my astonished eyes, she started grinding her pelvis with undulating movements. She watched herself closely in the mirror, sliding the silky cloth back and forth over her pussy. At last her entire body collapsed up against the mirror, the magnificent breasts crushing against the screen. I could almost feel her hot breath fogging the glass, feel her breath on my cock, which was stiff and hurting with desire. I was dying to free it from my pants and milk it hard and fast... but what if someone came in? To make things worse, the beautiful stranger kept stroking herself with the cloth, faster and faster. I rubbed at my crotch through the thick fabric of my pants. I wasn't used to this kind of lone pleasure — especially not at work! — and was having trouble relaxing and letting go. Wasn't I the guy who everyone trusted to respect the anonymity and privacy of women? I was none too pleased with myself. But in spite of everything, my hard on was becoming a monster. "My" customer spread her legs slightly, put her finger right in the middle, and started moving it with a steady rotation. After only a few moments, she closed her eyes and her entire body arched with pleasure. My hand between my legs, I was just about to undo my zipper when the office door swung open. It was one of my colleagues wanting to know if I'd had lunch. Red with shame, I leapt to my feet to hide my customer from the intruder. I mumbled that I'd be down in ten minutes and told him to wait if he wanted. My excitement wilted to nothing. What a close call!

That evening I tried to convince Margaret to come to bed very early. I said I was tired and needed to feel her close, but that she could read if she wanted. She got into bed with her back to me. I slid over to her side, as close as possible. In a flash I had a fabulous hard on... Margaret pretended not to notice. She excused herself, got up and went into the bathroom. Ten minutes later she came out again with curlers rolled tight into her hair, and the same old dreary night cream on her face. She gave me a little kiss on the forehead, lay down much too far away, and fell asleep a few minutes later. Disappointed, bitter, frustrated, I went into the living room and turned on an idiotic sitcom. I went to bed hours later, after spending half the night dozing on the too-hard sofa in front of the TV.

* * *

Saturday, October 15, I was glad to be working only until one o'clock. I was tired and irritable from my bad night and was in no mood to kid around with my co-workers. I went straight to my office, avoiding the cafeteria. I thought I was home free until I saw Nicole coming down the hall with such a bright smile and shrill, cheerful voice that I felt a terrible headache coming on.

— Hi, Paul! Having a bad day?

— I'm fine! I snapped, without meaning to.

— Hey, take it easy... You seem a bit frustrated.

She was nobody's fool, that Nicole...

— No, just a little tired.

I was dying to ask her about "my" customer. Did she know her? What was she like? What kind of voice did she have? Was she going to come today? What was her name? But I managed to hold myself back, and escaped into my office with a thermos of strong black coffee for company.

The hours passed and she didn't appear. I was very disappointed but at the same time relieved. I realized this woman had become an obsession. I thought about her the way you think about a lover, longing after her, trying to be satisfied with what little she wants to give you, craving a kiss, even a smile. I felt totally ridiculous. Totally miserable. My shift ended, and she hadn't even bothered to stop by.

Sunday, October 16 was a day of complete mediocrity. I spent the day in an almost feverish state. All I could think about was her, daydream about that splendid body, her hands stroking her pale skin, silky hair tumbling down over her shoulders. I missed her. I felt like an addict in withdrawal from just one day of not seeing her. All I could do was wait for the next day, Monday, a day so quiet it was almost dead. She was sure to come break the monotony, brighten the day with her presence, I just felt it! I had no concrete reason for thinking such a thing, but I was convinced.

That Sunday morning I left my house, got in my car, and drove to the Fashion Gallery. No, I wasn't working that day, but the store was open. Who knows, maybe she'd be there. I'd thought of sitting quietly by the door, maybe having a bite to eat and watch people come and go. And if she appeared, what would I do? I'd be happy just to look at her, I'd be satisfied for the rest of the day. I would finally know all those details I was dying to know: the exact shade of blonde her hair was; the colour of her eyes; what perfume she wore. I could follow her without being seen, pretending to do some shopping for my wife. And what would I say to the employees I ran into who knew I had no reason whatsoever to be there on Sunday? I'd think of something...

By late Sunday afternoon, I was still there waiting. I ate a sandwich and waited. I drank a cup of coffee, then another, and waited. At four o'clock, bitterly disappointed, I decided to go home, pathetic and ashamed. Just by chance, Margaret had to go out that evening, leaving me alone with my obsession. And that's what it was. For the first time in ages, I took the rum bottle from the cupboard and poured myself a good shot to try and forget her, or at least make the next day come faster... I drank more than I should have, and Margaret had to wake me up as I lay passed out on the sofa. Luckily I'd had the sense to zip up my fly before falling asleep in an alcohol haze. The last thing I remembered was fumbling to wash my hands after coming all over myself, my pants rolled down over my hips, imagining Her kneeling in front of me, welcoming my cock into her beautiful wide open mouth.

* * *

On Monday, October 17, I got up with the dawn. I was ready for work ridiculously early, which made Margaret suspicious.

— What're you up to this morning?

— Oh, you know! It's busy at the store. There's a meeting to talk about the shifts over Christmas. I'd better get going...

Another lie. This was definitely becoming a bad habit. But I was so excited I couldn't stand it, I just wanted to get to work as fast as I could, sit down at my station and wait for "my" customer. There were still hours before she arrived, many long hours to wait... Monday morning was usually pretty deserted and boring. Everyone knows that nothing happens on Mondays. But I didn't care a bit. There I sat, waiting for her visit, ready to welcome her and savour what little of her beauty she was willing to share with me.

I was pleasantly surprised to see her arrive around ten. Maybe she wasn't working that day?... What exactly did she do for a living, I wondered. She could have easily been a model, but I had other ambitions for her. I imagined her as the head of a big cosmetics firm, or maybe a fashion magazine. But none of that mattered. There she was in front of me, that's what counted. What's more, she didn't seem in as much of a hurry as usual. She strolled up and down the aisles, examining a jacket then a pair of pants. She tried on a magnificent fur coat and admired herself in the mirror for a long time, wrapped in soft fox pelts. She looked like someone who wanted to buy herself a treat but was hesitating. Could she afford it? She continued on her way, this time stopping at the fine jewellery counter. The Fashion Gallery prided itself on its vast assortment of precious gems and gold. She tried on pearl necklaces, diamond rings and bracelets studded with tiny emeralds. She lingered a long time in front of some earrings that I couldn't see in detail, but which were glittery and obviously expensive. Then she moved on again. She seemed to be wandering with no precise goal. Suddenly her face lit up with a sweet smile. A tall, impeccably dressed man with a self-assured step was coming towards her.

My heart skipped a beat. What I fool I was! How could I be so upset by the sight of this spectacular woman with an equally spectacular lover? It wasn't like I'd been hoping to have her for myself! This impressive man was a world apart from my humble self ! He was massive, I was small. He was slim, I was chubby. He had thick wavy black hair, mine was greying and getting thinner all the time. I wouldn't stand a chance with a woman like that, and it was stupid even to imagine it.

The couple headed for the fine lingerie section. Coquettishly she showed her companion some of the ensembles she'd tried on. The man slowly walked around the displays, selecting a few items and handing them to her. His taste was less subtle than hers, to say the least. She seemed to prefer clothes that were chic and attractive, not crass and suggestive, but he preferred the sort of thing that left nothing to the imagination. He held up tight corset tops that looked uncomfortable but exciting, and tiny g-strings with matching garter belts. She laughed, they laughed together and kissed... they seemed happy. Well, at least someone was happy! She took the most daring corset top and a g-string with garter belt, and headed into one of the fitting rooms. Before my eyes, my angel from heaven would soon be transformed into a far less respectable woman, and the idea gave me an instant hard on.

When she got to the fitting rooms, she went to Nicole and they had a long conference in low murmuring voices. They giggled and exchanged knowing looks, glancing over at the man, who seemed to be having quite an effect on little Nicole. My angel entered the dressing room and I saw Nicole go over to the shoe department. She chose a pair of thigh boots with dizzying high heels and brought them back, leaving them in front of fitting room 8, where She was already getting undressed.

This time, she seemed to be in a hurry to put on the items chosen by her lover. I watched admiringly as she stood naked before me, not taking the time to look at herself, but grabbing the bustier, whose small waist made her breasts bulge out provocatively over the top. The stiff fabric made her waist seem tiny, while making her voluptuous hips look rounder. She tugged hard, almost frantically at the strings in front, lifting her breasts until the nipples popped out the top. Dazed, I reached out to the screen, hoping to touch those plump, full curves that offered themselves sadistically, driving me out of my mind! She slipped on the tiny g-string. Why had I never noticed that the Fashion Gallery sold such get-ups?... But what a nice way to find out!

She hooked the garter belt around her waist and attached the silky stockings she was wearing when she came into the store. She looked at herself in the mirror and seemed pleased by what she saw. She quietly opened the door, picked up the boots that Nicole had kindly left, and gracefully pulled them on. She was breathtaking. I was in heaven, I could barely contain myself — and that was just the beginning.

My beautiful customer loosened her hair with a skillful gesture, and her magnificent blonde curls tumbled down over her shoulders. Then she rummaged in her purse and took out a tube of bright red lipstick, rouged her nipples then applied it to her lips. She spun around and I admired her magnificent derriere to my heart's content, the almost exaggeratedly round buttocks, the slender thighs snug in the soft leather boots, her tiny waist... Then she opened the door to her lover.

He examined her closely, had her pivot, admiring his choice of clothes and their full effect. Then he entered, closing the door behind him, and took her in his arms. He kissed her with hungry passion, caressing, pinching and kneading her delicious buttocks. His hands moved over my beauty's tender flesh, and I let my own hand do what it was aching to do. I seized my stiff member and watched the couple. She was perched on a little stool and swung her breasts in the man's face. He took hold of them and freed them from their tight confinement, greedily licking off the lipstick. Then he pushed the g-string aside, freeing my customer's hot bush, teasing her pussy with an impatient finger. She threw her head back and played with her breasts, allowing her companion to multiply his caresses. He bent even lower in front of her, lifted one of the booted legs onto his shoulder and licked the bared sex. I could almost hear the beauty's moans, feel the shudders that ran through her body as her lover hungrily ate her. Then he stepped back, spread the sweet lips, and flicked his stiffened finger back and forth over them. She grabbed his hair, wild with excitement, and smiled as he shoved his finger into her over and over. She let herself be penetrated this way for a few moments before adding her own finger to the sweet torture. She stroked herself violently to the rhythm of the penetration, then suddenly shuddered and collapsed, her eyes closed.

The man took advantage of the moment to pull down his pants and jerk off. It was strange, he was going at almost the exact same rhythm as me, but that was okay by me. He brought his big cock up to her hair and plunged into it. At that moment, she opened her mouth wide and sucked him into her, kneeling before him, submissive. She seemed to know what she was doing, drawing almost his entire member into her hot mouth, taking a breath before sucking on it again. She sucked so hard I could see the movement of her cheeks, it was painful. I wanted her so badly it hurt, I wanted to take her this way, watch her do what she was doing to this man, but to me, do it with her dressed the way she was and in the place where she was doing it.

I could see very well, too well, the man's reactions, his cock growing bigger and harder with her strokes. He gripped her head, forcing her to take him deeper in her mouth, and she did not resist. He made her go faster and her head was a blonde whirlwind, then suddenly he interrupted her, turned her around in front of the stool, and made her lean forward, still on her knees. He got behind her and entered her in a single stroke, with such force that her head hit the wall. Her back arched and she spread her legs further apart to receive him. I had an excellent view of his big pole entering her. I could almost feel, with every thrust, the muscles of her sex squeeze around my own cock. I was so excited I thought I was going to come without even touching myself, but instead the tension just mounted all the more.

The man stood up and grabbed my beauty by the hair, pulling her to her feet. She let herself be manhandled without saying a thing. In fact, she seemed to like her lover's roughness. He pinned her wrists on either side of the mirror, and I could have sworn she was looking at me. There she was in all her splendor, all mine, helpless, her eyes wild, with a little veil of sweat glistening on her upper lip. The man got behind her. Perched on her dizzying heels, she was almost as tall as he was. She pushed out her buttocks and shimmied her upper body even closer to the mirror so her breasts were crushed against the screen. I watched, hardly daring to breathe. Suddenly he took her, hard and savage, crushing her breasts and face against the mirror to the rhythm of his thrusts. Any harder and she'd have gone right through the mirror and land on my lap... And I'd have been ready for her! I was harder than I could ever remember being, and I pumped my poor member to the rhythm of their lovemaking. She looked like she was in another world. Eyes closed, mouth open, She made a superhuman effort to stifle the cries that would have alerted the other customers. He thrust harder, deeper. I could feel they were close to coming, and so was I. Suddenly the lovers were taken over by a sort of frenzy and they went faster and faster, going from passionate to unbearable. She opened her eyes, damp strands of hair sticking to her face. She didn't look much like the sophisticated and elegant woman I'd been fantasizing about for five days. She had become a tigress, a whore, out of control. She was as wild as he was, thrusting her hips and pelvis in a dance of ecstasy until they both reached a massive climax. They fell onto the floor in each other's arms, kissing, exhausted and completely satisfied.

Meanwhile, at my station, I surveyed the damage. An incriminating stain on my pants and a huge puddle in my hand, which wasn't big enough to hold my flood of pleasure. I made sure no one was lurking in the hallway, and sneaked into the washroom to clean myself up. I came out a few minutes later, dazed but happy, floating on a cloud of images that I'd never forget and never tell anyone, but keep to myself for future pleasures.

"Ah! She spoiled me!" I said to myself. "If she'd known I was watching, thing's might have been quite different."

Margaret sometimes tells me I'm a sucker.

I pretend it's not true, but she's right.

In the weeks to come, she wasn't the only one who called me a sucker.

It started Tuesday morning, the day after I got fired.

That was the day after Nicole and her gang stole over $800,000 worth of merchandise from the Fashion Gallery store that I was supposed to be guarding.

The day they robbed the store while two accomplices made love in a fitting room.

The headlines read: "Voyeur security guard duped..." and other captions like that.

It happened Monday, October 17.

Nothing ever happens on Monday...

"Dear Julian"

"*Dear Julian,*

I saw you play at the Crystal Club last Saturday. You were spectacular, as usual. My girlfriends told me I should go talk to you, try and get you interested, but I just couldn't. Not that I haven't thought of it!

I know I'm your most faithful fan. You must have tons of them... but not like me, I can tell you.

I get in this state every time I see you. It's something about your face, your look of being in another world, your hands stroking your guitar strings, or your sublime talent. I love to watch your long fingers move up and down the neck of the guitar, feeling its every vibration, making it live and die... Something about you puts me in a trance. Nothing else exists. There's no other sound, no other image. I'm not in a noisy bar any more, there's no more smoke, or people. I float in a sort of bubble where there is nothing but you. Just you, your faraway eyes and your music.

Maybe next time I'll finally go talk to you... But I don't know. For the moment, all I dare do is let you know that I exist. That somewhere out there, there's a woman who is dying to meet you, who would be crazy with joy if even one of those songs you bring to life was inspired by her.

But I'm getting carried away. Forgive me. For now I'm content just to find out where you're playing next, go watch you, admire you... desire you.

See you soon,
X"

Julian could not believe it. Nothing like this had ever happened in all of his career. Though maybe the word "career" was a bit strong to describe his music. This music, which in fourteen years had earned him barely enough money to pay his rent and eat, had brought him far more worries than glory. This music, which he had never been able to give up, had even cost him Janelle.

He crumpled the letter into a ball, then thought again. What man would let himself throw a letter like that in the garbage? It was probably from a girl barely old enough to legally enter the Crystal Club... or some frustrated woman who had no other, more direct way of showing interest. Still, he could not hide his pleasure. And why should he? He had never — at least, not as long as he could remember — been the object of such admiration from a woman, not even Janelle...

They had met in one of those trendy bars where he sometimes played with his band. He noticed her right away, but could not think of any intelligent or coherent way to strike up a conversation. True, he was used to women making the first moves, even if it never amounted to much — especially in that kind of place... But Janelle had not even looked at him. Then later, during the show, Ian, the singer, had asked if anyone in the audience wanted to come up and "sing the blues". Janelle had gotten up on stage with an air of confidence, and flashing him a smile that could have melted an iceberg, started to sing.

That was when he started to feel the first signs of love at first sight. His hands grew damp, which interfered with his playing. His head started buzzing, and it wasn't because of the thundering percussion a few feet away. Suddenly there was so much adrenaline pumping through his body that he almost thought he was having some kind of attack. But no, it was just her.

To make a long story short, the evening ended much better than it had begun. Around 2 a.m., Julian was madly in love with a girl he knew almost nothing about. All he knew was that she had no dark secrets that could spoil everything, no husband or other problem lurking on the horizon... She was the woman of his dreams, and they had lived together for over four years.

He pushed these memories away before they became painful, and went back to his admirer's letter. Despite the memory of Janelle and the pain she had caused him, he could not help but feel a little flicker of flattered curiosity.

A few days later he received another message.

"Dearest Julian,
Last night, you were even more enticing than usual. This time it was your hair that set me on fire, not your hands. The lighting made your curls shine... I imagined them brushing over my face.
I never see you with a woman, Julian. Did someone hurt you? Or maybe one woman isn't enough? Last night, I imagined you naked on that stage. I saw you alone beneath the multicolored lights, your body bathing in an orgy of colours, and me next to you, secretly admiring you.
Soon I'll be brave enough to introduce myself. I just need to know that your body and heart don't belong to anyone. If I could be sure of that, I would give my whole self to you...
See you soon, Julian.
X"

Well! She wanted to be sure his heart did not belong to anyone! In spite of himself, this sentence took him back to his four years of almost complete happiness with Janelle. Happiness that was so stupidly interrupted...

At the time, he had managed to provide for their needs, but she was painting and selling more and more of her work. She started reproaching him for not buying her treats the way she did for him. When he tried to reason with her about an overpriced vacation, pointing out that it would be wiser and just as much fun to stay close to home, she accused him of being selfish. She said he did not love her enough to "make a few little sacrifices". In other words, he did not earn enough money and did not prove his love to her the way he should, while she just grew richer and more generous... Everyone knows that women are perfect — it goes without saying! But her attitude became unbearable. Then came the day she accused him of playing with his "sleazy little band" just so pretty young women would come on to him.

That was the last straw. For the first time in four years of living together, she had stooped a little too low, dealt the ultimate insult, refusing to understand Julian's deepest motivations. He had never given her reason to believe he could be unfaithful. Never! He never even looked at another woman, knowing that his other half was a little possessive, and touchy. What's more, he was still madly in love with her. Being a pacifist, he preferred to avoid unpleasant discussions... and anyway, she was always so sure she was right.

Two months ago, she had given him an ultimatum: either he got himself together to have a more "normal" life, that is, with a bigger income and guaranteed presence after 10 p.m., or he found another apartment and someone else to share it with.

For once, he stuck to his guns, no longer feeling the need to justify his lifestyle. He left without a scene, without protests. But the drawback was that he missed her terribly. For the first while, he had to restrain himself from trying to patch things up. Then, when he got no sign from her, he became resigned. Maybe it really was time to turn over a new leaf...

For two weeks there was no news from his mysterious correspondent. But he was not performing as much, either. Julian started to think that his mysterious fan had found someone else when, coming out of the dressing room of a seedy bar one night, he saw a letter with his name on it stuck to the door.

"Hello,
Forgive me for being out of touch, but I missed your last show. That'll never happen again! Maybe you think I'm a little strange, or that I hide behind these letters because what I have to show isn't too appealing. Believe me, it's not that... And you're going to find out for yourself soon...

I have to go now, but this is not goodbye... See you very, very soon.
X"

* * *

It was a big night for Julian's band and their future. Six groups were appearing at the Spectrum, and there were supposed to be some big industry names scouting the event, looking for the next hit band. All the members of the group were very nervous, but it was a positive nervousness. They had spent part of the day setting up, each group making sure they would have the best possible sound when their turn came. They tried as best they could to relax backstage, when Andy, who worked the front door, came and knocked. He handed Julian a letter and gave him a little wink. Julian leapt from his chair, and when Andy confirmed that yes, the mysterious stranger had really been there, in person, he pressed him for a description.

— Oh, I don't know, you know me... A girl. Sort of tall. She was wearing one of those caps, so I couldn't see what colour her hair was. And sunglasses, so... But she seemed nice, for a girl...

Andy was not much help. He was gay and proud of it, and said that for him, all girls looked alike. Exasperated, Julian ripped open the envelope.

"Hi Julian,
I'll be with you tonight. I'll be looking at you and thinking of you hard. I know you're going to be a big success... it would be too bad if we couldn't share it. And who knows, maybe tonight will be the night? I'm going to think it over during the show. But I promise, you won't be disappointed when we finally meet. So til later, maybe. In any case, see you soon.
X"

Julian reread the message several times. He hoped she would make an appearance, especially if the show went well. If it didn't, he would be in no mood to make conversation with a stranger — a stranger who was probably not his type at all.

Finally he put the envelope in his guitar case with the others. "We'll see," he told himself.

Julian tried to concentrate on the upcoming show. The other band members were running through the various tunes to avoid any possible glitches. But Julian's mind was elsewhere. Maybe this woman would make him forget Janelle once and for all? Janelle, whom he had loved in spite of her mood swings and low sex drive. At first it upset him, how rarely she had given herself to him. But he had to admit, when it did happen, it was unforgettable, though she had no particular imagination and did not go in for sexual games. Still, she made love with such unusual abandon that it was endearing and quite moving.

He came back to the present, trying once again to bury these painful memories. Maybe, after all, he would be pleasantly surprised by his new admirer...

He was still asking himself these questions when their turn came to go onstage. The band members patted each other on the back for encouragement, it was a sort of ritual they did on big nights, then took their places on stage. The atmosphere was electric, the place was packed. The crowd greeted them with enthusiasm, and each musician threw himself into bringing his instrument to life.

Right from the first bars, Julian felt invincible. "This is why I play music!" he told himself after a piece they had played particularly well. The audience was going wild. It was turning out so well, Julian felt an almost sexual pleasure. If Janelle had ever had this kind of feeling, this kind of exaltation while doing her art, she never would have acted the way she did! Adrenaline kept him on a highwire, honing his nerves to a keen sensitivity that came through clearly in the music. During his guitar solo in the final piece, he felt like a god and was ready to swear he had never given such a good performance. He suddenly realized he was lucky to have his guitar in front of him... The erection that had been building since the beginning of the show was at its peak.

The five musicians left the stage amidst thundering applause. "We've got them!" they congratulated each other. Nobody dared to say anything out loud, but their smiles spoke volumes. When the crowd called for an encore with insistent applause and chanting, they flew back on stage. The tune they played seemed as successful as the ones before, and Julian was even more excited. His member manifested its satisfaction by getting even bigger and harder.

When they left the stage for the last time, the musicians were all charged up. With only fifteen minutes to clear their equipment off the stage, they hurried into the dressing room for a moment's celebration.

Julian was the last to leave the stage, so no one realized he was no longer with them. A woman he could not see had grabbed his arm and dragged him into a dark closet. A door closed behind him. He tried to protest, but she planted her wet mouth on his. And what a mouth! An avidly probing tongue invaded his lips. Avid, but at the same time shy... like a barely contained passion. The kiss seemed to last several minutes.

— Julian, please don't go...

The voice was soft, almost a whisper. Without giving him the chance to reply, she started kissing him again. Julian's erection, which had lost none of its vigour, suddenly went up another notch. Was this woman his mysterious correspondent? What did she look like? Her kisses were very pleasant, but he did not relish the idea of discovering she weighed 300 pounds and had the face of a witch! He put out his hands hesitantly to touch her body. "Hmm! not bad! My hands fit nicely around her waist, that's a good sign... at least for that part of her." He let his hands slide down her hips, and found only pleasing curves.

The strange woman, encouraged by his gesture, grew braver. With a well-placed thigh, she checked how Julian's crotch was reacting, and was not disappointed. Her little hands grabbed his buttocks, moved down the back of his thighs, then around front where they started to undo his pants.

— Hey! I've got to go back...

— In a minute, she whispered.

She moved down his body gradually, with furtive kisses on his damp neck and chest. Julian took advantage of the moment to slide his hands onto the large, firm breasts, which seemed very cramped in their tight shirt. "Looking better and better!" he said to himself. But he really had to get backstage. How to escape the situation, which was far from unpleasant? "What man would be stupid enough not to jump at the opportunity?" he thought with conviction, to ease his conscience.

As for the girl, apparently she had already "thought it over", and was going for a very specific goal. Having finally succeeded in pulling down his very tight jeans, she seemed to want to tame his cock, now free and unencumbered, with mischievous little flicks of the tongue. Julian moaned. The guys could get along okay without him, he thought, and his conviction was confirmed beyond the point of no return when the greedy little mouth swallowed him whole, licking him with a very wet tongue, letting warm soft saliva trail down the full length of his member.

In one last gasp of lucidity, Julian groped for the hair of his benefactress, to smell it, get an image of her, even just a sketch. But she was wearing a big cap, a kind of beret. Maybe her hair was very short, or very long and tucked up under the cap? Whatever the case, she knew what she was doing! And she really seemed to want to torment him. After a few minutes his cock was streaming, and the girl's hand took over. With her light fingers, she delicately massaged his testicles, separating them tenderly before squeezing them against each other in a burning embrace.

— I'm sorry, Julian, but I can't wait any more, she murmured.

— That's... that's okay, really. But why are you hiding like this?

— I'll explain one day.

She concluded by taking him between her lips again, right into her throat. He felt himself buried deeply in her, too deeply, even. He was astounded by such ardour, but was not about to complain. Especially since it was the kind of thing Janelle always refused to do for him... He thought of how strange it all was: there he was, locked in a broom-closet with a perfect stranger sucking him like he had never been sucked in his life! And it was happening to *him*! Now!

As if to convince him of it, the girl grew more insistent. She sucked faster and harder. Her hand went back to stroking his testicles, which felt as if they were about to burst. In a frenzied series of gliding and sucking movements, she managed with little difficulty to make the man she was pursuing explode in a powerful stream, flooding her benevolent mouth.

Julian tried to catch his breath. He felt the stranger pull away. There were so many questions he wanted to ask her! But they would have time, later... Even before his breathing went back to normal, he saw light coming in through the opening door, felt her slip by him, and realized too late that she was gone.

The episode could not have lasted more than a few minutes, ten at most, but Julian could have sworn it was hours. Hours of intense pleasure... He remained in the dark locker for a moment to recover, asking himself if it had all been a dream. But his twisted pants and quivering cock were proof that it had been quite real. He did not know how to react. He was not about to complain that he had been used! No, his pleasure had been too great. But he knew nothing about what his benefactress looked like. "At least her body wasn't bad!" he concluded with a smile. And most importantly, he had come with surprising intensity.

Julian quickly pulled up his pants, ran an uncertain hand through his tousled hair, and headed backstage.

Seeing him arrive, the other musicians jeered:

— Where were you? The fans wouldn't leave you alone?

— You have no idea how right you are! replied the guitarist with an enigmatic smile.

They left the little room, and Julian sat down, opening himself a beer. He wondered when the stranger would make another appearance. He was sure she would show up any minute. But by the time he had finished his brew, she still had not arrived. He got to his feet with some difficulty, wondering if it was the show that had drained him or what came after...

He joined the others on stage, quickly gathering his equipment to make room for the next group. He took another beer before going to clear his things from the dressing room. There he met Alan who asked him, surprised, if he was leaving right away. Julian replied that he would put his equipment in the car and come join them right after. But Alan, who had noticed his strange smile earlier, could not help but ask:

— Was it our performance or something else making you smile like that?

— You'll never believe what just happened to me. I was leaving the stage, and...

— C'mon, out! Gotta make room for the next guys!

One of the organizers had just come in, interrupting Julian as he was about to divulge his secret. They all ended up at the bar and spent the rest of the evening drinking, congratulating each other, drinking some more, listening to the other bands, and drinking still more. Julian searched the room, hoping at any moment to see a pretty girl in a cap. But the stranger was keeping a low profile. At the end of the evening, the beer had extinguished what remained of the bonfire in Julian's crotch, and he stopped looking for the girl. Quite drunk, he told Alan about his happy misadventure, though he was no longer sure it was not just a dream. He told his comrade the story in as much detail as possible and listened to him exclaim in jealousy.

Leaving the bar later that night, he wondered if he should not have just kept quiet.

* * *

After that evening, things started happening very quickly. Julian's group was offered an attractive recording contract. There were fewer shows, as the musicians preferred to prepare for the record. Julian thought less and less about the strange woman and her very pleasant favours. He hardly believed it had really happened... except at night, when he longed for her between the sheets. She had shown no sign of life for three weeks. Had she been disappointed? Had he done something wrong? But it had been her who did everything! Maybe that was it, she was waiting for some sort of reply from him... But she had left! So too bad for her!

Julian had no idea that at that very moment, she was talking on the phone with Alan. She wanted his help for her next surprise visit to Julian.

— Hi, Alan. It's Janelle...

— Janelle? Uh, hi... How are you?

— Fine, fine. Listen, as you might have guessed, I'm not calling to talk to you about my health. Did Julian ever tell you about something unusual that happened the night of the Spectrum?

Alan was silent for a few moments, remembering the outrageous tale Julian had told him the night of their last show. He had only half believed him.

— Then it was true? It was you?

— I don't know what he told you, but yes, it was me. Maybe it seems like a strange method, but I have my reasons. I miss him so much.

— Listen, Janelle, I don't want to be involved.

— I know. The reason I'm phoning is that I'm going to Quebec City for your next show. I'd like to spring another surprise on him, more elaborate this time, if you know what I mean... After that, he'll know it's me.

— Janelle, he's just starting to get over it. You're not being fair...

— That just concerns him and me, Alan. What I want you to do is very simple. Let me in backstage after the show, and make sure everyone gets out. I know Julian always waits a few minutes before going back out, to "decompress"...

Alan thought for a few moments.

— It might work... But you've got to be there the moment we finish. If he comes back right away, it won't be my fault.

— I'm just asking you to try.

* * *

Just when he had stopped waiting, Julian received another letter from her. He could not help smiling idiotically, remembering, down to the last detail, the treatment she had inflicted on him.

"Dear Julian,
It's been very hard to get in touch with you lately. I almost thought I'd never see you again! That would've been too bad, I think you'll agree. I hope I measured up to your expectations the other day... I did my best to make a good impression!
I won't tell you why I didn't stay the last time, it's not important. But I'll be in Quebec City for your next show. Maybe we'll have a meeting as nice as the last one — or nicer?
Until then,
Love,
X"

Quebec City. She would be in Quebec City... Julian adored that town. Besides being beautiful, it was warm and alive — anything could happen there. And maybe, just maybe, "everything" would! He was almost jumping out of his skin with impatience. He forced himself to calm down, thinking about the unpleasant things that could happen:

- Maybe, as he'd feared, she was as ugly as a toad, in which case he would regret having let his impetuous cock venture into that mouth, but would file the episode away as a "lapse of judgment";

- Maybe she was totally unbalanced and would threaten his life if he wasn't attracted to her;

- Maybe it was some kind of bad joke, the kind only women knew how to play. He had been chosen by chance, a helpless victim.

There it was. "Is that all? The risks aren't *that* bad!" he concluded. "And if she does what she did last time, what's a little humiliation compared with so much pleasure?"

* * *

Once they got to the hotel in Quebec — though "hotel" was just a fancy way of saying "seedy-room-with-sagging-mattresses-as-usual" — the musicians, according to ritual, drew lots to decide who would have the supreme privilege of a room to himself. Julian was the lucky one this time, and he felt this was a good sign. They quickly showered then headed to the venue.

By 10 p.m., the place was packed. Local radio stations had done a publicity blitz for their arrival in Quebec, and gave them star treatment. But though the show went well, it did not have the magic of the last one, as if the musicians were trying too hard, or their minds were elsewhere. But the crowd did not seem to notice, and they got two standing ovations.

Julian was impatient. He liked to play, he loved the tension and the spectators' appreciation. But he could not stop thinking about what would happen after the show. Would she keep her promise? He had no reason to doubt her, and knew he should take her at her word. He did his best to maintain the illusion of being totally absorbed in the music. When the show was over, he did not follow the others right away, preferring to remain in the wings. He told himself if he waited there, it would make things easier if she meant to drag him into some dark corner. But ten minutes went by and she still had not appeared. He decided to go back to the dressing room. He met the other band members on their way to the bar, where they were awaited by some tall cool blonde brews, and, if they got lucky, maybe some tall hot blonde fans as well...

— Are you coming, Julian?

— I'll be there in a minute.

— Come now, our fans are dying to meet us!

Julian resigned himself to going for a tall frosty one before getting changed.

* * *

The dressing room was locked. Each musician had been given a key and was told only they would have access to the room. He opened the door and fumbled for the light switch... which was covered with adhesive tape! The door closed behind him. She was there, putting a hand on his shoulder.

— You knew I'd come, she whispered.

— I was hoping...

— Oh! So you liked me the last time?

— I'm only a man!

He guessed she was passing in front of him. She took his hand and put it on her naked shoulder. The young man shivered. Was it possible she was wearing no clothes? She guided one of his hands to her naked breasts, placing the other on the hollow of her hip. The male hands touched smooth flesh, soft as velvet, whose proportions, at least to his blind palms, appeared perfect. He felt long silky hair tumbling down her back... he loved long hair.

She went to him slowly and gave him a long kiss. She tasted of mint. Pulling his shirt out of his pants, she patiently unbuttoned it, then rubbed her generous bosom across his hairy chest.

She murmured into his ear:

— You're going to know who I am very soon, but before that, I want to taste you. I've waited for so long! I promise you won't be disappointed. I'm trying to be different so you'll always remember me, in case I never see you again.

— But why? Why wouldn't we see each other again? he whispered.

— Only you know...

With these words, she took one of the man's fingers and brought it up to her mouth. She licked it, sucked on it languidly, then brought it between her legs.

— See the effect you're having on me?

— You're having the same effect on me... but the guys are going to be back soon, and...

— No they're not, I took care of everything...

Their words were almost inaudible, charged with urgent desire. He smiled in the darkness. He was ready for anything, and had never been so hard in his life. He told himself once again that he should take advantage of this pleasant distraction, which would probably be short-lived. If only it were up to him... He conjured up a picture of the young woman and was suddenly filled with doubt: what if it was all a serious mistake? But his body told him it was too late to think: time to act! He explored the thighs that offered themselves to him, and the mysterious place between them. She was wet, even juicy. Completely shaven, every inch of her sex was exposed to his probing finger. He caressed her for a few moments and she pulled him to the floor, lying him back on the rug. A leg that felt long and slim shoved between his thighs, discovering his cock in all its vulnerability. Her hair tumbled down over him, tickling him from face to knees, lingering over his groin. A velvety tongue slid over his skin, leaving a trail of sweet saliva.

She sucked him between her lips and into her open throat. She was talented, using just enough pressure with her hand and just enough suction with her mouth. It was delicious, and the man felt his organ grow almost a whole inch longer. She sat up and stroked him with her slippery hand. He guessed she was rubbing herself with her other hand. There was no other sound but the sound of her breathing, which was more and more rapid. He felt the vibrations of the woman's hand on her body, and the mounting pleasure she was giving herself. He felt her climax approaching, sensed her body straighten up and grow totally still for a few moments, then relax. She had come in silence, without giving him the chance to participate in or share her pleasure. But she quickly recovered and went back to stroking him tenderly. Straddling over him, she put him inside her and sat down on him, impaling herself. Remaining still for an instant, she leaned over and gently kissed him before starting to move her hips with a regular, lazy movement.

He was her victim, with no control over the situation. Not that he had any intention of trying to change anything! He was being spoiled! Someone other than himself had taken over the wheel. She hovered over him, light and supple. She got up on her heels so that she seemed almost weightless as she moved up and down over the man's body. A little higher, a little lower, ever so gently.

He felt himself being pulled backwards. She had turned around. Still gliding, but more insistently, she took him by force, mastered him. Her sex crushed against his pelvis, making him softly cry out. The young man wanted to get on top of her and show her what he was made of, but she guessed his plan, and seized his arms. She led him to the door and tied his hands behind his back with a scarf that had materialized from somewhere. How had she found it in the darkness? He had no idea, and actually, did not care in the least.

Tied to the doorknob with his cock pointing forward, the victim had no other choice but to let his assailant have her way. On all fours in front of him, her thighs squeezed together, Janelle forced him inside her from behind, making him go faster and faster. She was like a wet, warm velvet pouch inside, squeezing and crushing his cock mercilessly. His torturer's buttocks smacked against his belly, her long hair flew back against his sweaty face. He did his best to control his thrusts, to keep rhythm with the woman's movements, trying to force himself upon her. He felt he was close to letting go, but wanted the sweet torture to last a little longer. She had other ideas. Leaning on her elbows and spreading her legs, she shoved back against him, charging and squeezing him in the most intimate embrace until the man, unable to hold back any longer, exploded inside her with jerking shudders of pleasure.

She hurriedly undid his bonds and dragged him back down on the floor, huddling against him. He did not know what to say, and anyway, his throat was so dry it was impossible to speak for the moment. He was completely subjugated, stunned, speechless.

His heart had barely gone back to its normal rhythm when they heard a key in the door. He cried out:

— Wait a minute! Give me a minute, guys!

The couple leapt to their feet and scrambled to find their clothes on the floor.

— Come on, let me in, I want to change!

That voice... Janelle felt her stomach turn. Was it possible...?

— Come on, Alan, that's enough! I'm coming in!

Janelle felt as if she had been hit over the head. Alan? Impossible... But wasn't that Julian's voice on the other side of the door? At that moment Julian entered, letting in just enough light for Janelle to recognize him.

Brigitte's Secret

$\mathscr{B}$rigitte looked at her travelling companion, half sceptical, half flabbergasted.

— You're not serious?

— Totally.

— I'll have to think about it...

— Don't take too long.

She thought about it, trying to get used to the idea he had so candidly suggested. "Well, I guess it's possible," she said, then nodded.

She thought back on the week they had just spent together. Brigitte had come to Mexico to work. Since she did not have to go to work until around 10 p.m., she spent her days lying in the sun, letting her skin drink in the warm rays.

The man had appeared the first day of her trip, a lone jogger struck down by a cramp or some other problem. He was hunched over, wincing, with his hands on his knees, obviously trying to ease the pain. She thought he was truly suffering, and hurried over to see if she could help.

— Are you okay? she asked in English, not wanting to make a fool of herself with garbled Spanish.

He looked her straight in the eyes and smiled broadly.

— And you even speak English!

It took her a few seconds to realize she had been tricked. Pretending to be annoyed, she exclaimed:

— That's not very funny! I thought you were really in pain!

— No, not at all, but you have to admit, my approach was original!

His innocent smile was irresistible, like the smile of a little boy caught red-handed who knows he's done nothing really wrong and will be forgiven. And Brigitte did not hold it against him... he was a very handsome man. Tall and muscular without looking pumped-up, he had a superb suntan that accentuated the sweat gleaming on his skin. His hair was jet black and like a perfect vacationer or seasoned charmer, he had not shaved for at least two days. His radiant face with its beautifully sculpted features sported a dark five-o'clock shadow. His piercing eyes were the same colour as the ocean. The man exuded sexuality.

— If I go for a dip you won't run away, will you ?

She shook her head. The man pulled off his tank top and ran into the warm ocean waves. He swam out with a strong front crawl, dove into the foamy breakers a few times, then came back out. Brigitte had gone back to her chair.

— You got here yesterday...

— That doesn't sound like a question.

— It's not, I saw you arrive. We're staying at the same hotel. Are you here for long?

— Just a week. But I'm not really on vacation, I'm working.

— Pretty nice work!

— The best!

— What do you do?

She had been waiting for this question. It always came up sooner or later. But she had no intention of revealing the nature of her work to this Adonis! He would probably mumble an apology, then think up some excuse and leave. They all did, at least the interesting ones. So instead she answered:

— I'm a model for a Montreal fashion designer. I do private shows for certain customers. It's not as exciting or prestigious as magazine work, but it's pleasant, even if I do mostly work at night. And it allows me to travel.

This was not so far from the truth. She actually did do shows, but not modeling clothes. Quite the opposite! Brigitte was an "exotic dancer". A stripper... and she loved her work. Unfortunately, and this was her only regret, some of her colleagues gave her profession a bad name. But most of them did not do it in the same conditions or for the same reasons as her. Brigitte danced for pleasure. For practical reasons too, of course — after all, it paid very well, the hours were flexible and she could travel. But most of all, it allowed her to satisfy a powerful need to unveil her charms for the eyes of an admiring audience.

The first time she danced was on a bet when she was a student. She had gone to a strip bar with a few friends who had dared her and two other girls to get up on stage and strip. The sum of the bet grew with the boys' desire to see their classmates take their clothes off. Within minutes the stakes had become quite interesting for a penniless student. But Brigitte quickly realized that even without the money, she would have done anything to get up on stage in front of her friends. She was drawn by some undefinable instinct... Yet she had never given it a thought before that moment. The idea pulled her like a magnet. The two other girls finally declined, leaving Brigitte to rise to the challenge alone. With an air of determination, she knocked back her drink and got up on stage in front of her amused companions. They were sure she would just do a quick little appearance, take off her clothes and hurry off the stage — a joke was a joke. But much to their surprise, she firmly planted herself at centre stage. With the first bars of the music, she took off her shoes, then her blouse. She spent the entire song taking her clothes off one piece at a time, until she stood there completely naked.

At that moment she realized she was totally in her element. Sensing people's eyes lingering on her body gave her enormous pleasure, as if she were being caressed by countless hands. On every inch of exposed skin, she could almost taste the heat of each penetrating gaze.

That first night, for those few minutes, she couldn't have been more excited than if her four friends had made love to her one after another.

Unfortunately, the girls stopped talking to her. As for the boys, they all asked her out, hoping for a free private show. But she swore that she would never let a spectator touch her after seeing her perform. That would destroy the dream illusion she created when she danced. And she had no need for more attention. She loved the keen sensation of desire that came from the men, and sometimes the women too. All those eyes pinned upon her made her shiver with pleasure, and she gave herself to the dance, body and soul. She knew she was beautiful, desired. She knew most of the men would give everything they had to make love with her. But the ultimate pleasure was that she had never spent the night with a customer! To continue enjoying her work, she had to remain totally inaccessible to her audience. She had to remain a fantasy, a mirage. That way she could become any woman she wanted, queen or movie-star... "Look, but don't touch!"

In short, she was happy with her work. However, it did have its down side. Some people, once they discovered what she did, stopped seeing her because they could see nothing meaningful or socially acceptable about her "career". As for the wives and girlfriends of the men who came to see her dance, they despised her. But that did not bother Brigitte too much, as she never came face to face with any of them. Still, to preserve her anonymity, she always worked as far as possible from home, refusing all contracts near her residence. At long last, she had succeeded in making a separation between her work and her social life, and she meant to keep it that way.

Luckily, the line about being a "model for a Montreal fashion designer" usually went over pretty well — this time too, for the man did not press for more details.

— What about you? she asked him. Are you on vacation?

— Yes... I have to go back to Montreal in a week. Do you live there too?

— Yes... In the suburbs.

— I feel as if I've seen you someplace.

— Montreal's a big city.

They were silent for a few moments. Then, as if remembering something important, the man got to his feet and with an almost solemn air said:

— I'm sorry, I haven't introduced myself. My name is Vincent. I'm thirty-four, single and I am dying to ask you out to dinner. What time do you start work?

— Not before nine. If you don't mind eating early, I'd love to join you... I'm Brigitte.

— No problem, we can eat early. Let's say we meet in the lobby around five...

The conversation had taken a relaxed, easy tone without either of them really noticing. It was clear they liked each other. Brigitte joyfully accepted his invitation. Vincent was happy and once again flashed his dazzling smile.

— I'm going to get on with my run... without stopping this time. See you later!

She watched him go with a strange feeling in her stomach. She liked him, she liked him very much.

* * *

Brigitte went to meet Vincent at the agreed time. She was wearing her most beautiful dress, which was white and brought out her golden tan. She had taken meticulous care with her hair and makeup. After all, she was a model! Vincent seemed to appreciate her efforts. He got up from the chair when he saw her, whistling with admiration. He himself had taken pains with his appearance. Or was it his natural charm? He was clean-shaven and gave off a dizzying though subtle perfume. He did not ask her where she wanted to go, but simply took her to his rented vehicle, a convertible sports car parked at the door.

— It's good for cruising women, he said, winking.

— Yes, I guess I'm not the first one to get into this car in the last few weeks!

— No, but you're definitely the most beautiful!

He opened the door and closed it once she was settled. He took his place behind the wheel and asked her if she liked seafood. At her obvious approval of the idea, he started the car.

It was a carefree drive, full of good humour and light banter. They arrived at a little restaurant. It looked quite unassuming but Brigitte recognized its name from the tourist brochures, which raved about it. They were shown to a little table on the almost empty terrace. As Vincent seemed to know the place, Brigitte let him order. He spoke a near-perfect Spanish and seemed to be ordering enough food for an army.

The conversation was lively and joyous. Brigitte could

not help but admire the young man sitting across the table. He was magnificent. But — and this didn't harm — he was also funny, intelligent and could talk about almost anything. She learned that he had his own public relations firm, had been coming to this place for the last four years, and had never been married or even seriously involved with someone. He was looking for "the" ideal woman...

The evening went extremely well, but too quickly. For the first time in a long while, Brigitte did not want to go to work. At least, she would have delayed going if she could have. She wanted to spend the rest of the evening — and who knows, maybe the night — with this man she felt she had known for years, though they had only just met. But when she imagined the feverish eyes of the audience slipping over her naked body as she danced, she shuddered with pleasure. She looked discreetly at her watch and saw she would have to leave soon. And there was no question of him giving her a lift! Even a hint about what she really did could ruin everything.

Vincent also knew she had to leave. But how he wished the evening could last forever! Could he see her later?

— What time do you finish tonight? he asked her softly.

— Oh! Around two in the morning. My boss has rented a reception room and the party will probably go on late.

— That's too bad... I would've come to meet you for a nightcap.

— I definitely won't be back before three a.m... I'm sorry, I'd have liked to stay. It's been a wonderful evening...

— I totally agree, the most beautiful evening I've had in a long time! Well! I guess we'll have to start again tomorrow night, won't we?

— Or even before, if you want. I get up pretty early...

— Perfect! I'll be on the terrace for breakfast around ten. How about you?

— I'll be there!

Reluctantly they got up from the table and left the restaurant. He took her gently by the arm, guiding her to the car.

— I'm going to take a cab...

— I won't hear of it!

— No, I mean it. I have to go to the other end of town, there's no point! I insist.

— Well, just this once...

He pulled her towards him, and before she could do anything to stop him — not that she had the slightest desire to do so — he kissed her with such passion that she went limp in his arms. There were so many promises in his kiss! His firm body drove her wild and his smell went straight to her head. She gently pulled away and whispered:

— I'll think of you all evening.

— And I'll think of you all night... I haven't felt like this for a long time. I'm already crazy about you!

Again he pressed his tender lips against hers. After a seemingly endless embrace that left them both glowing with desire, they managed to tear themselves away from each other. Vincent went into the restaurant, called a taxi, then came back and took her hand. They waited in silence. When the old taxi pulled up, he helped her in, gave her another burning kiss, and watched the vehicle pull away with a somber look on his face. For the entire trip, Brigitte wondered over and over if this man could accept her life as it was. He seemed so sensitive to beautiful things and refined manners, to a woman's softness and delicateness... he would no doubt be horrified to learn where she was going and what she would be doing for the rest of the evening.

* * *

She arrived at her workplace with only a few minutes to spare, and hurried to get ready for her first number. She could not stop thinking of Vincent, the softness of his lips, the heat of his kisses. As if floating on a cloud, she got up on stage and started her first dance. The bar was crowded with Mexicans and, most of all, with American tourists and businessmen. It was quite a chic place and the clientele was decidedly upscale. Brigitte had been told that the customers rarely got out of hand or made trouble, so she felt completely secure. She stepped forward on the stage, wearing a sequined bra and a matching g-string, perched on stiletto heels. Her graceful body started to move to the rhythm of the music. Gradually she transformed into the goddess she became each time she got on stage for the pleasure of her audience.

Her movements became more and more languid, as if her body were there only to be admired and desired by the spectators. The audience was attentive to her every move, each man looked at her with a certain glimmer in his eye. She asked only to be possessed, devoured. Her long legs seemed to go on forever, her open thighs displayed her almost totally shaven blonde bush. She finally took off her top, letting her long hair caress her back and tickle her breasts deliciously.

All she could think of was Vincent. She wanted him there admiring her. For all the men who were looking at her now, she was nothing but a dream. They faded into nothingness next to Vincent. She imagined his hands running over her body, massaging her ample breasts, spreading her thighs to discover her hot pussy that longed only for him.

At the end of the number, Brigitte hurried off stage, as if waking up from a dream. She fled to the bathroom. Her breath came in gasps, she could not help but think of Vincent. Her dance had made her very excited, the many eyes on her firing her desire. Reaching down between her legs she caressed her damp sex, and in only a few seconds came with a long sigh.

* * *

The next morning, she went to the terrace at ten. Vincent was already waiting for her with a glass of orange juice in front of him. He got to his feet, his face lighting up with his incomparable smile. Brigitte did not look quite so fresh. She had slept badly, dreaming about Vincent, his body next to her in bed... then on her, and in her. She had almost broken a record for masturbation and had to force herself to stop, more frustrated than ever. But now seeing him there in all his magnificence, in the bright morning sun, her good mood instantly returned. Fearing she might be ill at ease after the way they had separated the night before, Vincent was determined to reaffirm his intentions. He did not even give her time to sit down, but took her in his arms and kissed her with as much conviction as the day before. All she wanted was to suggest they go have breakfast in his room, but something prevented her. He seemed to emanate a deep respect that would not allow things to be hurried between them.

They ate in near silence. Their smiles spoke volumes about how they were both feeling. After a bountiful meal they decided to head for the inviting beach. Vincent knew how to do everything. He introduced her to the joys of undersea diving, sailing, and parachuting. He seemed to have a natural aptitude for everything physical. Brigitte pondered about this aptitude, impatient to see just how far it went. But indeed, Vincent seemed to be in no hurry. She would have liked to suggest a little afternoon nap, but again held herself back. If he wanted to make her wait, why shouldn't she do the same?

They went swimming, splashed each other and played like children. Around three in the afternoon, exhausted, they decided to nap... but not the kind of nap Brigitte was hoping for! They each went to their room, agreeing to meet again around 5 p.m. for a drink and dinner. Vincent was definitely more difficult to corrupt than the men Brigitte was used to. How refreshing!

* * *

The alcohol went to her head. Brigitte was becoming obsessed. As Vincent talked over drinks, she examined his jaw and his teeth, and every time he moved, she admired his muscles working beneath the tanned skin. He seemed to be doing the same with her. They were in a world of their own. They had hamburgers and fries for supper, washed down with several margaritas. When the time came for Brigitte to leave, she was very tipsy and so was Vincent. But at least that way she had little trouble convincing him to let her take a taxi again. The trip in the shaky old vehicle did not do much to sober her up. But the effect was not unpleasant, and she ordered another drink when she got to the bar, before going off to get changed.

When she got up on stage she was very lightheaded, but not just from the alcohol. She felt so well that her body seemed to dance by itself without her having to give it orders. All she wanted was Vincent. Yes, she would soon have to talk to him about her work, though she was surer than ever that he would not let the woman of his life practice this sort of occupation. He had the look of someone who was used to controlling situations, not having them forced on him. Something in his look gave her the feeling that this time she might have to choose. But she banished the thought, content just to enjoy the present moment. That evening, several men asked her to dance at their tables and paid generously for the favour. She even danced for a couple of lovers who seemed to revel in the spectacle. She liked these private dances, for they allowed her to get dangerously close to the limit she had set for herself. She could look people in the eye, guess their secrets and their fantasies... but it was a one-way street. She kept up her face of marble, her motionless smile — the image of an inaccessible goddess. When she danced for a man alone or at a group table, she thought of Vincent. How she would have loved to show him this side of herself! But it was impossible... She was madly in love with him and that would not change, unless he did something to gravely disappoint her in the next few days. He would never understand that she could do this work and also have a simple healthy life, totally free of the "vices of the trade". It was so hard to explain to someone on the "outside"! But this man seemed to represent so many promises... The more she got to know him, the more he resembled the Prince Charming she had been looking for all her life. Was it possible she had finally found someone for whom she would even give up her work, give up this pleasure that had become so important to her? Maybe... She would just have to see how things went.

* * *

When she got back that night, Vincent was waiting for her. The hotel bar was closed, and he was sitting in one of the armchairs in the lobby. He looked as if he were dozing, but when he saw her come in through the big front door, he leapt to his feet and in a single bound was before her, taking her in his arms.

— I... I just had to see you...

Leaving her no time to answer, he crushed his mouth against hers almost painfully. Taking her by the hand, he led her to the elevator. Staring straight ahead as they waited, he seemed to be concentrating very hard on something. When the elevator doors slid open with a pneumatic hiss, he grabbed hold of her again and pushed her inside. She fell back against the wall. Vincent pressed himself against her, took her face and hair in his hands, and kissed her passionately. She felt his insistent body pushing itself against hers, leaving no doubt as to how much he wanted her. He ran his hands over her body, discovering each of her curves with greedy delight, crushing her back and breasts with his powerful arms.

The doors opened at the fourth floor. Without a word, he took her to his room and feverishly threw the door open. In an instant, they were both naked and breathless, mute with desire. They did not waste a second, but collapsed on the thick plush carpet. Vincent plunged into her with no warning. Pinned beneath him, Brigitte could barely breathe, but her desire was so intense that it did not matter. She wrapped her long legs around him, forcing him into her hard, clutching him into the depths of her body. Then she rolled over so she was on top of him, now forcing her desire upon him, her insatiable mouth, her conquering sex that squeezed him tighter and tighter. They kissed as if they had been waiting for years to accomplish this simple gesture, joining their tongues and their saliva, exploring each other's mouths almost desperately. He penetrated her roughly, unrelentingly, and the woman thrust her hips flat against him, pushing him away then pulling him in deeper. Gasping for breath at the brink of orgasm, they pulled apart for a moment, then plunged back into each other. When neither could hold on any longer, they came at almost the same instant, Vincent flooding into his companion in utter silence.

They remained this way until the brink of sleep, then dragged themselves to bed, sinking happily into the sheets before sleep finally overcame them.

Several hours later, Brigitte was awakened by a delectable sensation. What she assumed was a tongue was tracing abstract shapes on her back, trailing down and tenderly tickling her buttocks. Vincent massaged her head, his fingers tangled in her silky hair. Gently he turned her over on her back so he could lick the front of her body. From her ears he went down her neck, then lingered over each breast before getting to her belly. He kissed her thighs, knees, calves, feet with light, almost furtive kisses. Brigitte lay still, fully savouring these superb caresses. When Vincent spread her legs and slid his tongue inside her, she gave a nervous little jump before giving into the pleasure.

His patience was the complete opposite of their first lovemaking hours earlier. He nibbled her gently, happy to hear her sighing beneath his mouth. With a tender gesture, he spread the engorged lips of her sex so he could get to that most vulnerable place in her body. He darted his pointed tongue inside, teasing Brigitte's slightly bruised and swollen flesh. She swam in a sea of pleasure, body and spirit floating. Her body came alive with what felt like thousands of tiny sparks, she felt herself vibrate. Fingers came to replace the man's tongue, pushing deeply into her, making her moan with pain and pleasure. Then the skillful tongue began its caresses again while the hand plunged deeply inside her, bruising her flesh even more. The hand felt Brigitte's sex trembling on the verge of violent pleasure. Vincent slid on top of her, then inside her, plunging with ease into her wet pussy, prolonging the precise and regular gliding movement that rubbed at the open lips, bringing forth new moans.

Brigitte felt herself melting like an ice cube in the sun. Her lover filled her. He slid into her slowly and deeply, letting his member slide to the inmost depths of her body. It was if the hard and pulsing organ was truly a part of herself.

Their breathing became more and more uneven, each adapting to the other's rhythm in a dance of lust. Leaning against the head of the bed, Vincent made her sit on him, bringing her breasts to his open lips. She floated on top of him, obeying only the arms of this man beneath her hips who dictated their rhythm with the full length of his member. Looking Brigitte deep in the eyes, Vincent pressed his probing hand between his companion's thighs, seized the sex that begged to come again. At a single touch from him, Brigitte exploded with pleasure, and when Vincent caught his breath sharply a second before he came, she was convinced she was madly in love. She never wanted to leave him. Ever.

* * *

That is how they spent the rest of the week. They made

love from morning to evening, stopping only to take advantage of the sun or take a dip in the warm ocean. After sunset, they walked on the shore, looking for the perfect place to give free rein to their desire.

On the last evening, Vincent took Brigitte to the top of a cliff overlooking the bay. The air was sweet and fragrant, the grass silky. They both wanted this last evening to remain an unforgettable memory. They got undressed slowly, exposing their naked skin to the moonlight and the delicious breeze. Kneeling before each other, their gestures tender as if in prayer, they brought each other to climax in silence. Lying beneath the starry night sky, they made love for one last time on Mexican soil. They fell asleep wrapped around each other, completely satisfied, and did not waken until dawn.

* * *

Vincent changed his plane ticket. He was absolutely determined to go back on the same flight as Brigitte. Once he had made the change, he went by his companion's room and knocked.

— Can we talk?

— Of course! About anything you want!

Brigitte playfully tried to lure him to the bed.

— No, this is serious.

She thought she could see a dark cloud on the horizon and was afraid. She sat down on one of the armchairs and listened attentively.

— Brigitte... this last week has been extraordinary.

— Yes, but...?

— But? There is no but! I just wanted to know if we could keep seeing each other once we're back in Montreal.

I mean, just the two of us. I couldn't stand it if another man touched you or even looked at you... So if you have someone else in your life, or if you aren't ready for this, just tell me, please...

Without hesitating, Brigitte got up and slipped into his arms. But she was racked with anxiety. She had thought he wanted to tell her about some other love he had in Montreal, and she would have had to accept it. Not without shedding a few tears, but she would have had no other choice. At least then he would have been the jerk, not her! She had to be honest with herself: she adored this man and sooner or later would have to explain the true nature of her work. But how to explain to the man you love that you dance for people just for pleasure? She didn't take drugs, she had no financial problems, contrary to all the clichés about exotic dancers... She danced for her own pleasure, for the sense of power and confidence it gave her. How to admit to the man of your life that you need to feel devoured by the eyes of others, to feel their desire? She decided to delay this revelation. Anyway, during the past week, she had gotten to know him and understood that he would never agree to her working the way she had done until now. He had a way of seeming almost possessive...

She would find the right moment, or another solution.

* * *

Finally they left their hotel to go to the airport. After the usual formalities, they boarded the plane and made themselves comfortable in their seats, side by side. The take-off was smooth, and because it was a direct flight they would be seeing a film after they ate.

It was just after the meal that Vincent made his first advances.

— I want you so much.

— I want you too. When we get to Montreal, let's go straight to my place. You don't have to go back to work until tomorrow...

— I mean I want you right now!

He slipped his hand under her little meal tray, then under her short skirt. Immediately Brigitte felt her own desire come to life. The hand wriggled into her panties and quickly found what it was looking for. She was already very wet.

He pushed a finger into her, it was almost painful but she was ready for him. Vincent discreetly seized one of his companion's hands so she could feel his own state.

— Let's go into one of the washrooms!

— They're way too small! Besides, we'll get caught. It's impossible, and you know it.

— No it's not! Come on, I can't wait any more!

— Just wait until they put on the film...

Under the cover of their meal trays, they caressed each other with increasing ardour. When the flight attendant came to take the trays away, Vincent had just enough time to cover his swollen member and remove his wandering hand before they were seen.

Right away, the lights went down. Vincent got up, kissed Brigitte on the cheek and asked her to come with him. The couple made their way to the back of the aircraft. Luckily, the washrooms were unoccupied. Brigitte let him go ahead of her into one of the narrow little cabins, then, throwing caution to the winds, followed him in.

* * *

Vincent was leaning against the tiny sink and welcomed

her with open arms, locking the door behind her. Their embrace was passionate, reigniting the sensations they had been giving each other for the entire last week. The cabin was quite cramped, but they were not about to complain. They wanted to be as close to each other as possible.

Pulling up her skirt and switching places with her companion, Brigitte managed a bit awkwardly to perch on the little counter. The faucets pressed painfully into her buttocks and released a little stream of warm water, but the discomfort was short-lived. Vincent did not waste any time, but pulled down his pants, seized his companion's thrust-out hips and plunged between her widely spread thighs.

Just as they had expected, someone knocked at the door.

— Can't they read, it says "occupied"!

— Don't worry, there are other washrooms.

— But how are we going to leave after? Everyone will know.

— So? They can't throw us out of the plane, can they?

Vincent put an end to her objections by crushing his lips against hers. Then, pulling back, he knelt down in front of her and kissed her coppery, wet bush. She immediately stopped protesting and let herself be rocked by the movements of her lover's tongue. Turbulence and the vibrations of the aircraft made his movements a little clumsy, jerking his mouth away from her only to thrust it back upon her. When he felt she was ready to come, he stood and plunged his sex deep inside her. Brigitte's soft cry was muffled by the constant rattling in the washrooms.

Her legs wrapped around him, she pushed him into her with wild impatience, biting his powerful neck. By moving to the far edge of the sink, she could even put her feet up on the wall on the other side of the cabin. With every thrust, Brigitte's head bumped against the wall behind her, but she was barely aware of it, absorbed by her pleasure. Vincent was breathing more quickly now, and she came in a torrent only seconds before her lover.

They remained in each other's arms for a moment, then started straightening themselves up. Her cheeks were pink and her eyes bright; his breath was ragged and his hair disheveled. They decided the best way was to emerge together and head back to their seats, looking innocent. But when they opened the door an elderly lady stood there waiting, looking them up and down in disdain. However, two young men sitting in the back row next to the wall of the washroom gave them a thumbs-up sign.

Brigitte blushed furiously, while Vincent merely smiled.

* * *

The rest of the flight was without incident. After getting to Montreal, they stayed at Brigitte's for a few days, then at Vincent's. It was clear they could not get enough of each other, far from it. But at the end of the week, just before Brigitte had to go back to work, she knew it was time to tell him what she did and why she did it. She spent three days agonizing, wondering how he would react. She was so afraid her confession was going to change their relationship! She hesitated, procrastinated. Finally she made her decision. She would tell him the following evening, the night before she went back to work.

Vincent was out, and she spent the whole day getting ready. She wanted everything to be perfect: champagne, gourmet meal, soft music... First she would tell him how important he had become to her. Then she would tell him that she had not been totally honest and it disturbed her.

She wanted a stable, monogamous relationship with him, so they had to be as honest as possible. *Voilà!* If she put it that way, how could he hold it against her ?

Next she meant to explain that this work she had been doing for years made her very happy, but that she was ready to give it up if he really could not accept it. This last part was painful, but she had to face it: she would, in fact, give up her work for him. A future with him seemed so full of promise! And if that is what he wanted, he would surely give her time to find something she liked to do just as much — even if she had to go back to school! Besides, his financial situation seemed more than comfortable...

Vincent would no doubt be happy she had trusted him enough to tell him everything. So why was she almost sick with anxiety? Because more than once, she had seen disdain in the eyes of people she liked and respected when she told them what she did for a living. And she would not be able to bear that disdain, coming from him. Anything but that! She tried to convince herself that he wouldn't react that way, he was open-minded and not so puritanical as to condemn her for such a thing! But she was wringing her hands with worry. For of all possible scenarios, this one was the worst. She could take it if they broke up, or if she had to change professions, but to see the man you love looking down on you...

Anyway. It was too late to change her mind, Vincent would be there any minute. Brigitte paced the apartment obsessively, enough to wear out the rugs! Vincent was late. He chose his moments! She had told him clearly that tonight was important, that she had something to tell him... Why was he late?

To calm herself down, Brigitte turned on the TV to the

73

six o'clock news. The newscaster was just reading the headlines:

— Armed robbery in a branch of the Royal Bank.

— Major drug bust at the Toronto airport.

— Montreal police arrest suspect after a three-month search.

She only half-watched the first two stories. The third made her heart skip a beat. Vincent's photo appeared on the screen while the newscaster's voice droned on:

— Vincent Logan, thirty-four, was apprehended today after a three-month intensive police search in Mexico and across Canada. The accused will appear in court on charges ranging from procuring the services of a prostitute to running a common bawdy house. Police tracked him down after he was seen at Mirabel airport last week...

Brigitte could not believe her ears. "And I thought my secret was going to ruin everything!"

WHEN OUR FRIENDS LET US DOWN...

$\mathscr{I}$t was a week night and the bar was almost empty. I'd been in the city two days and didn't know anyone, not a single living soul I could share my recent happiness with. And I felt like having a drink to celebrate! I had been on cloud nine since the day before I left home. I was just starting to realize that you sometimes have to go through a rough patch to really appreciate the good things in life... I sat down comfortably at the heavy oak bar, leaning on my elbows and patiently waiting to catch the eye of the sympathetic looking man working behind it. I didn't have to wait long. When he brought me my scotch, he noticed the glow on my face. He said it was nice to have such a happy looking customer for a change. He asked me what was up. I asked him how much time he had. Looking around the desolate bar a bit gloomily he said:

— All night!

I couldn't resist. I got right to the point.

— Until last Wednesday, I'd been suffering for eight months. Exactly 252 days, 252 mornings, noons, evenings and nights. Eight months and a few days of worry and hell and living with a feeling of unreality and total emptiness. Thirty-six weeks of agony and existential crisis. Why, you ask? Because my best friend let me down. He'd been my friend forever. We spent the happiest moments of my teens and adult life together. He was my friend, my brother, almost a mentor. He was the one who introduced me to pleasures I can't even describe, and allowed me to explore them as much as I wanted. He was my moral support, the one I could always count on when times were tough, and he could always count on me. In fact, he took my loyalty so much for granted that he turned me into his toy, his slave. Without him I was nothing, I was worthless. I even wondered if I could really say I existed...

— Your friend went away?

— Went away? No... not at all. Because I'm talking about *him*, of course... The one who's been hanging between my legs since I was born and controlled me since my fifteenth birthday or so. My thing. My tool. My cock. My dick. My pistol.

You see, the bugger didn't want to get up any more. I tried everything... I've known him awhile, you know, and I know the kind of thing that turns his crank. But even the juiciest situations left him totally indifferent. He just hung there, totally limp, not even daring to look me in the face. I reasoned with him, I sweet-talked him, but nothing worked. I stroked him, I played with him, I tickled him... nothing! I even tried to stimulate my brain which, despite all my beliefs to the contrary, is supposed to control the sex drive and send the right message down to our buddy... but still no luck.

— Gee, I'm really sorry.

The bartender had a funereal look on his face, even more than if I had been talking about a real friend who had actually died. He shivered with dread and asked me:

— And it happened just like that? Without warning? Had it ever happened before?

— It happened overnight. First time in my life. And I'd never wish it on anyone! If you want me to tell you about it...

— Oh, yes! It's not the type of thing that's ever worried me, personally, but I'm curious. A person can never learn enough about that type of thing!

— You're right about that! Myself, I wouldn't have panicked so much if I'd heard anyone talk about it before... But where to begin?...

First I'll tell you a bit about myself and what that wonderful organ meant to me before it, or some cruel destiny maybe, decided to play that dirty trick on me.

For two years, I've been with a stunning woman. At least, I was with her until recently... She's three years older than me and very understanding — up to a point. And she's what I'd really call a knockout. So, this woman was the first I'd had a so-called stable relationship with. I mean, for two whole years I never slept with another woman and she didn't sleep with another man, at least, as far as I know. That's about as close to True Love as I've ever gotten. Before her, of course, I'd explored the various possibilities the female gender had to offer, with all its adorable qualities. I can even say I tried everything I wanted to try, with as many partners and as many types of women as I wanted.

As I was saying these words the man, who had been nodding understandingly up until then, gave me a look of the deepest respect.

— You see, I revere women as a species, whether they're blonde, brunette, red-headed or even going grey; tall, short, thin or chubby, all women hold a mystery that every man, with a bit of skill and luck, should try and uncover.

— I couldn't agree with you more. So tell me, have you uncovered any good mysteries you'd like to share?

— I've got hours and hours of stories! But the best... No, wait... Ah, yes! There was the time I got a very sophisticated massage from the hands of two pretty Oriental women. I say "hands", but actually it was their entire body... Picture this: they covered me with almond oil then started sliding over me like eels, one in front, the other in back. I saw hands everywhere — between my buttocks, over my cock, around my waist, in my hair — and their tongues slid into every corner. It was divine... Just imagine! You'd have thought they were competing to see who could give me more plea-sure. They were both tiny and delicate. After sucking, licking and groping whichever one of them was closest, I got to go inside them, one after the other. They were so small they almost choked my cock, but I wasn't com-plaining! I penetrated one while making the other come with my hands, then they traded places. I barely had time to see the face of the one I'd just mounted before the other took her place. And then when I was ready to explode, one would sit on my face and force me to lick her as hard as I could, while the other one tenderly massaged me so I could get my strength back and hold on awhile longer. Finally when she felt I was ready, she sucked me like mad. Then the game began again. I could barely make out whose mouth or pussy was wrapped around my cock... I don't know how I did it, but it lasted for hours. What sweet mem-ories! What incredible pleasures! My skin smelled like al-monds for weeks after...

The bartender let out a low whistle of admiration, then said:

— Maybe I got married too young... Do you have other stories?

— Oh, yes. I was in my heyday then...

I was quiet for a few moments, trying to remember. Suddenly Simone sprung to mind:

— I'll never forget Simone. Hard and mean Simone. She took me to her dungeon where there was a poor naked girl tied up and gagged. Simone was dressed like a real torture queen, whip in hand. She chained me up too. First, she amused herself by shoving her hand, then the whipshaft, inside that poor girl. I was fascinated by the whip going into her and how much it turned Simone on. She made her come several times this way, and I was really suffering. Then Simone untied me and ordered me to make love to the girl while she masturbated. There was no way I could refuse! I did what she told me to do, without balking. The poor girl was completely soaked and I pushed into her hard, like Simone wanted me to. I ploughed her as hard as I could while watching my Mistress. Her hand rubbed back and forth across her shaved pussy between whip lashes, and from time to time, to reward me, she gave me a few little well-placed strokes. It wasn't too painful... and the victim was utterly delectable. She was totally passive and endured her punishment without complaining, while Simone forced me inside her by every means and into every orifice possible. No one said no to Simone! When she felt the girl had suffered enough, she ordered me to make her, Simone, come with the whip handle. I obeyed her to the word, knowing she was totally unpredictable. When she'd had enough of this instrument of lust, she told me to enter her. I was still all slippery from the other woman's love juice. The girl watched me go with regret, begging me with her eyes to stay. Simone took pity on her. She went to the girl, allowed her to fondle her breasts and kiss her while I penetrated her, first with the whipshaft then with my fine-tuned cock. Simone had become the victim...

— You're joking...

— No, I'm serious! I can still feel the whip burns on my back...

— Where does this Simone live?

— I can give you her number... but I can't guarantee anything!

The bartender was looking at me with downright reverence. Obviously he admired me as much as he envied me. I continued:

— I almost forgot the time I found myself rolling around on a waterbed with my cock wedged between two huge breasts... They were truly gigantic! While her companion ploughed her without mercy from behind, she sucked me or rubbed her huge knockers around my dick. She pressed them against each other, making me a prisoner in a tunnel of silky flesh. When I came, her whole face was soaked...

— Okay, enough! I believe you! Don't tell me more. It's getting painful!

— Okay, okay. I never saw any of them again. I was just trying to demonstrate that my cock has never been shy. It's been lucky enough to do things that other men just dream about.

— You can say that again!

— Anyway... To continue my story, like a lot of guys, I discovered sex at around the age of eight. My grade two teacher was a tall redhead with glasses who always wore very short skirts. She had legs that went on forever, inflaming the imaginations of all the boys in the class. I don't really remember my first erection, but my first ejaculation is very clear in my memory. It was a Sunday afternoon and I discovered my eighteen-year-old sister getting dressed. She was standing in front of the mirror, totally naked, and was touching one of her breasts almost nonchalantly. Seeing her like that, I got a magnificent erection. But it was when she spread her legs and touched herself lower down that I suddenly felt my pants get all sticky. From that day on, my life took on a new dimension. I'd reached sexual maturity — well, maybe that's an exaggeration! Let's say my organs were mature, for the sake of accuracy...

My new friend gave me a conspiratorial wink.

— From that day on, like all young boys I explored my fantasies with innocent little tricks like trying to see under the dresses of our little friends, or watching the woman next door undress. Nothing special or original, but still, for a precocious teenager it opened the door to a number of possibilities.

But back to the woman I shared my life with until recently: Eve. It was with her, but not because of her — at least I don't think so — that my sufferings began. The first time, it didn't seem like anything to worry about. We'd had a bit too much to drink... I had a good excuse. But at dawn, to make up for lost time, I started stroking the warm body in bed next to me. I wasn't hard-enough-to-explode like I usually am in the morning. That should've been a warning. But I convinced myself that the slightest reaction from Eve would bring my member springing to life and ready for action. Except, well... She woke up, stretching like a cat, licking her lips with an enticing little smile, but as for my member — nothing doing. To my great distress, it refused to take any initiative and remained sound asleep. I could not believe my balls! What was going on down there? Because I was quite excited otherwise... My brain, even though it wasn't totally awake, should have been sending the right signals... But nothing was happening. At first, Eve just looked at my limp dick in amazement. That's understandable,

83

because this had never happened before! She smiled nicely and bent over me, caressing my neck with little laps of her tongue, then my nipples, my ribs and my groin. "Oof!" I said to myself. I was almost scared for a second. I was sure this familiar treatment would fix everything. Eve's mouth got to my cock and totally engulfed it. I closed my eyes, letting nature take its course. A few moments later, Eve raised her tousled head and stared at me. She asked me what was going on. She didn't look so much worried as scornful. I told her firmly that things were just fine, but she got up and went to take a shower.

I was in shock. I tried to imagine her body in the shower, her skin all slippery with soap. That should've done the trick... I thought of going to join her, soaping up a froth between her thighs then taking her hard from behind. That sort of vision always woke up the warrior in me. But this time, it was no use.

Hearing Eve turn off the faucets, I pretended to be asleep. I admired her as she walked across the room, naked and streaming. She got dressed slowly, bra, matching panties, silk stockings, skirt, blouse, jacket, and finally shoes... Usually this drove me wild. The clothes she wore to work were enough to make my pole stand straight up in my pants. But not that morning. Nothing could be done. After Eve left, I seized the traitor roughly, forcing him to look me in the eye, and berated him. The episode left me flabbergasted. Empty. Completely drained. You can understand, can't you? But still, I took it all with a grain of salt and told myself that it was a one-time thing and wouldn't happen again.

— But that wasn't the case...?

— Alas, that would've been too simple... A few days later,

Eve and I were getting ready to go out with friends. I hadn't tried anything for a few nights, I was too afraid of another excruciating failure. But that night, I really meant to get things back to normal, and my companion gave every indication of thinking likewise. I watched her get dressed, full of lust, noting that she wasn't wearing anything under her short skirt. She put on her high-heeled sandals. I didn't really want to go out any more, but she convinced me to be patient.

On that note, we left the house. For the entire evening, all I could think about was her exposed pussy under her skirt, beneath the table. How many times did I try to slip my hand between her legs under the table? Eve let me do as I liked, but at a certain point she closed her thighs and gave me my hand back. Once, I managed to touch her, and felt that delicious wetness on my fingers.

To my great delight, I finally felt some movement in my crotch. That little caress must have woken my lazy member. You can imagine how proud I was! I tried to tell Eve. I took her hand and guided it over my pant leg to my lap. But what bad luck! Just at the moment when her hand got there... pfft! Like a stupid balloon deflating. Still, she must have felt the last vibrations of my erection, because she smiled at me and signaled that she wanted to leave soon. But the evening went on and on. The conversation was more or less interesting, the jokes were more or less funny, but there we were hours later, still sitting at that damn table. I was losing patience and getting bored. I'd almost forgotten Eve's skirt, I was trying so hard to stifle my yawns. When we were finally able to leave, all I could think about was sleep. But my companion had other things in mind. When we got home, I had barely gotten in the door when she lunged at me, kissing me greedily. Sleep? Who needed sleep? She pushed me into the bedroom, rubbing herself against me, kneading my buttocks and back. She slid her thigh between my legs impatiently. When her hand moved down my belly to my crotch and there was nothing happening, she said we'd just have to try something else.

After lighting the two candles on our bedside tables, she turned on the radio. She had me lie down on the bed, then climbed up and started dancing over me. She slowly unbuttoned her blouse, grasped her breasts and freed them from her bra, caressing them and even licking them thanks to some kind of neck gymnastics. Touching herself roughly, she made her dark nipples stand up. They seemed to be looking at me, waiting for me to act. Pulling up her skirt, she opened her legs so I could admire her glossy pussy, and smell its sweet perfume from where I lay.

She took off her shoes and spreading her legs even more, slid her hand between her thighs, continuing the caress I had started a few hours earlier. I lay there not moving, taking in the show. She came a little closer, put one foot on my chest and the other on the pillows. Her pussy was directly above my face so I could see every fold, but was too far to touch her. Her legs prevented me from moving, and that's exactly what she wanted!

I watched with fascination as her finger slid inside, coming out wet and gleaming. I was waiting for a drip of her juice to fall on my face so I could taste it at last... but she made me wait. Her finger started working harder on her pulsing sex. I could feel she was ready to come, but she didn't. Instead, she straightened up and went to get an oval-shaped crystal flask with a rounded end.

Again standing over my face, she slid the flask inside her.

It went in easily, as if it had been made just for her. I knew her very well, and reached my hand up to her mound, searching with my finger for the little bump that would make her cry out with pleasure.

Seeing the flask sliding in and out, quicker and deeper, my finger finally found the spot and rubbed it gently. Eve was panting, on the verge of orgasm. I looked at her tenderly, dying to replace that vial with my member, but she gave me no chance. Grinding her pelvis so my finger moved more quickly over her, she finally came, spilling her pleasure onto my face.

— Even just talking about it drives me wild… did it work for you?

— Patience, I'm getting there. I could now see what lay ahead. Unlike some other women, Eve had to be penetrated with force to make her orgasm complete.

Impatient and out of breath, she tried to take off my pants. Her hands were shaky and she couldn't undo the buttons, so she begged me to help her. Except… I knew she wasn't going to find what she was looking for so desperately. Anyway, not for the moment. I had to do something, fast. To put off the moment of truth, I offered to make her come again. I tried to get her down on the bed, pretending to attack her with my wet tongue. I finally managed to convince her, and turned her over on her back, buried my face between her wet thighs and started, with skill and savoir-faire, to draw her back into the delights of the flesh. I also wanted my cock to react, to do the thing it had been "trained" to do, but to no avail. I tasted Eve's pussy, and she seemed to like that. Her nails raked my back and her thighs gripped my head. All of a sudden I got an inspiration, an idea that would surely provoke the desired reaction from my organ. I said to Eve:

"Talk to me, tell me what you feel..."

"I'm on fire... I'm flowing like a waterfall!", she said. "All I need is your big cock to fill me up! I'm going to come, I'm coming!"

As if by magic, my cock finally reacted. Shy at first, it finally stood up with pride. I hurried to undo my pants. I looked at it, the old familiar friend, ready for action. But just at the moment when its head brushed against Eve's thigh, the bugger did it again. It collapsed. I was devastated. I tried to hide it from my companion, but in vain. She saw its sorry state at almost the same moment as me. She sat up, wrapping herself up in the wrinkled sheet, and went into the living room. Despite my apologies, she was convinced I was seeing someone else.

— Typical, commented the bartender.

— Yeah... I told her it wasn't true and that I was just as concerned as she was about the situation. She didn't know how to react. She didn't want to get mad, but couldn't help it. She decided to go to bed, leaving me alone in the living room to chain-smoke a whole pack of cigarettes, asking myself over and over, "Why me? Why now?" I hadn't changed anything in my routine. I wasn't more stressed or anxious than usual. Nothing like this had ever happened to me before, and I was desperate. Finally I fell asleep on the sofa, tossing and turning all night. At daybreak, I saw that my stupid dick was just as flaccid as the day before. Even my incomparable, legendary morning hard-ons had disappeared. I had to find a solution! Maybe one of my friends had been through this before? I was in a hurry to find out.

— And I suppose they told you it'd never happened to them?

— Exactly! And that just made it worse! It was like I was

attacking their manhood by asking, but meanwhile there I was, I'd put myself out on a limb and bared my soul. They all said they made love almost every day. The rare time "it" happened was because of their wives or girlfriends! They said maybe Eve just wasn't doing it for me any more. When I told them that wasn't the problem, they told me I should still look elsewhere — without cheating necessarily, maybe a strip bar, or X-rated movies... anything! They told me I should treat myself to a big helping of whatever made me hard.

That suggestion sounded as good as any other. On my way home that evening, I stopped by the video store. Before I met Eve, I liked films where a leather-clad dominatrix worked some poor guy over and reduced him to the state of an object. I'd always been excited by the idea of an Amazon with a whip and bright-red lipstick jerking me off until I cried out for mercy. I chose a cassette that looked pretty close to that fantasy, and went home with a bounce in my step.

When I got in, Eve met me wearing a little lace teddy and holding two glasses of wine. She led me to the sofa and sat down next to me. She apologized for her reaction the day before, and asked me if there was anything she could do to help me get over my "problem". I showed her the cassette and told her my plan. Without a word, she went into the bedroom and came out a few minutes later wearing a leatherette bikini and tall high-heeled boots, carrying two leather belts. She tied my hands with one of the belts and put the cassette into the video player.

The film was everything I wanted it to be. A tall brunette threatened a powerless man with her whip, ordering him to lick her boots then her sex or else she'd flagellate him. Eve did the same. She knelt down over my mouth and forced me to lick her with my head turned so I could still see what was happening on the screen. The tall brunette forced one of her large breasts into the man's mouth, which Eve also did, almost suffocating me. After a few minutes of this, the man on the screen, fully erect, had his pants torn off. The woman stroked him, softly at first, then wrapped her whip around the man's stiff member. Her saliva dripped down the whip handle, her lipstick leaving long red streaks.

Eve took hold of my limp prick and started playing with it. With her expert mouth, she sucked, shook and licked it. She did it so well I felt a shock of electricity run through my cock. Encouraged, she sucked me harder, caressing herself at the same time so I wouldn't suffer alone. I admired her round buttocks, her spread thighs, her lips wrapped around my member. What a sight! The bikini top barely held in her breasts, which rubbed against my hip. On the screen, the man's face was crushed as the cruel beauty sucked him in by force. His prick was huge, but still the woman took him all the way down her throat. When finally the man came, covering the woman's face with jism, I felt my cock wilt. Eve raised her head, disappointed. I turned away in embarrassment.

My new friend was silent for a moment before he exclaimed:

— I can't believe it, you were really blocked-stiff... excuse the expression.

— That's okay. I guess it's appropriate. Anyhow, Eve carried on undiscouraged, as ever. The next day, we tried going to a strip club. Eve knew that not so long ago, I used to go regularly with my buddies. This time, she swallowed her pride and accompanied me. The bar was pretty much the same as others of its kind. We sat down by the little stage and admired the dancing beauties. One of them, while performing some fairly suggestive dance steps, took off her panties, which landed on my shoulder. Eve smiled at me, amused. The girl danced in front of me for a few moments, and my companion signaled for her to come closer. She handed her a bill, which the girl slipped into her g-string. She had huge breasts, a tiny waist, round hips and very long legs. Her hair was pinned up, and she wore nothing but a g-string, a little bra, and red shoes with very high heels. She brought her stool over to where we were sitting and started dancing for us, looking us right in the eyes. Her strip went slowly, to the rhythm of the music. Stretching luxuriously like a cat, she turned so I could admire the curves of her buttocks. Then she turned to face me again, so close that the tips of her generous breasts almost tickled my nose. It was all I could do to prevent myself from sticking my tongue out. She slipped her hands over the curves of her body, and finally unpinned her hair, which tumbled down her back. Meanwhile Eve was murmuring in my ear. She wanted to know if I liked the girl, if I'd like it if she came and joined us. Imagine! She suggested we invite her, asked me if a little threesome would excite me, if I'd like to see her with the other woman. Seeing that her words were having an effect, she added more detail. She said I could take the dancer from behind while she stroked her. After that we could switch...

When the song ended, Eve gave the dancer another bill and continued. She said she thought the girl had very nice breasts and that she would like to touch them. She said she'd never done anything like that, and that I would have to teach her. Or else I could have the other woman to myself, and she would just watch... My night with Simone came back to me, and I felt my cock give a little jolt. My brain was on fire with all these possibilities. I saw myself with these two beauties, taking them one after the other, and them giving me a little head in between...

The other song was coming to an end. I'd had enough of the dancer. All I wanted was to take Eve as roughly as possible. My orgy days were over, but that didn't mean I couldn't have my way with my girlfriend! Taking Eve by the hand, I dragged her into the car. I was planning to have her on the backseat, then and there. We had left the car on a sidestreet, in a parking lot that I knew was quite dark. I opened the back door and nudged a fully consenting Eve in front of me. Closing the door behind me, I freed her breasts and started biting them lightly, then groped under her dress looking for her pussy which, yet again, was free and unencumbered by any sort of garment. I didn't want to take the chance of waiting or making a false move. I undid my pants as fast as I could and stretched out on top of her... then almost burst into tears! No sooner had I pulled "it" out of my pants than it went soft again.

— I can't believe it!, said the bartender. Listen, you're starting to really worry me... After all that you've tried! Did it get better or not?

— Let me go on... After this latest catastrophe, as you can imagine, I was completely at a loss. Eve comforted me as well as she could, but nothing worked. I didn't know what to do. When we got home, I poured myself a double scotch, then another, and went to bed.

Monday morning, when I left my tender companion, nothing whatsoever had changed. I was in a pathetic state. At the office, around 1 p.m., my secretary informed me that a Miss Lyndon wished to see me. Miss Lyndon? I didn't know any Miss Lyndon. I told my secretary to show her to my office. I barely recognized her at first, though she often wore this kind of clothing: fitted suit, satin blouse, high heels, silk stockings. But her face was hidden by a huge hat trimmed with a little veil. She looked like she'd walked straight out of *Paris Vogue* or some other fashion magazine. The secretary retreated and Eve slammed the door shut. I looked at her in astonishment. She said she'd been in the neighbourhood and thought she'd stop in to see me. She crossed her legs, which pulled her skirt up on her thighs, exposing the rim of her stockings. I was mesmerized by this leg clad in silk like a second skin. She was wearing a garter belt the same colour as her stockings, and playfully pulled at the garters. Putting her leg up and planting the heel of her shoe on my desk, she revealed that she had truly adopted the habit of wearing no underwear. I swallowed painfully, understanding where all this was leading. She picked up a pen lying on my desk, and slid it under the silky rim of her stockings, showing me how easy it would be to remove them. Then the pen started playing in the very short hairs of her sex, then circled around the fleshy lips. The tip disappeared for a few moments then reappeared, wet and shiny. She absentmindedly licked the end of the pen, and asked me if her seduction attempt was working. I looked at my lap, and was overjoyed to see a little bulge. I gave her a mischievous little smile. She smiled back, and before I could do anything, she got on top of my desk, pulling her skirt up around her waist. She got down on her hands and knees and thrust her gleaming crotch in my face. Confronted with such exhibitionism, I picked up a little cylinder-shaped trophy from my desk, and inserted it slowly inside her. Her sex was at eye level and I could see every fold, watch the object go in and out of her, growing shiny with her love juice. I started going faster. Eve moaned and her hand went down to meet the trophy, moving on the tender head of her famished pussy. I watched her pleasure, almost hypnotized by the metal object sliding in and out of her. I was so absorbed that at first I didn't notice my full erection. When I finally got so hard I couldn't miss it, I brought Eve down from on top of the desk. I turned her around, pushed her face-down over the wooden surface, and grabbed her tightly. I rubbed myself against her divine body, preparing to conquer her...

— In your office!

— In my office... No windows, great soundproofing. I kissed her neck and shoulders, letting the blouse glide over her breasts, and pinched her nipples. I was so relieved! It was working! I told myself, if that's what it took, to make love only at the office, that's what I'd do!...

But that idea must have had a negative effect, because right away my dick went back to the wilted state it was starting to be in far too often. Eve leapt to her feet, straightened her clothes, opened the office door, and snapped, "Thanks, anyway, Mr. Brennan!" She left the office, leaving me there with the door wide open and my pants down around my ankles.

— Oh, no! Did anyone see?

— I don't think so. But if they did, I don't think it would've added to my humiliation... I was already destroyed! Eve kept trying for three months, and I'll always be grateful to her, even though it didn't work. She tried everything: sexy outfits of every kind, accessories, films that got wilder all the time. Finally, she just gave up. She grew more and more detached until we had to admit that the damage was beyond repair, and the situation wasn't about to change.

We broke up. Both of us were bitter and disappointed. But I couldn't ask her to keep on being patient and cooperative, because I seemed to be a hopeless case. She ended up calling me a coward because I refused to go to the doctor. But there was nothing wrong with me! I could still get it up, briefly, it was just at the moment of truth that everything changed! I still felt the same quiver when I was turned on, but then the sudden pressure-drop ruined everything. No way I was going to talk to the doctor about it! Hey, this was *my* manhood at stake! And if I couldn't satisfy my companion on demand the way I always could before, well, too bad. I would just have to try and get better alone.

When they saw how pitiful I looked, my friends finally admitted that their claims of "almost every day" and "four or five times a week" were not quite accurate. My friend Sid even admitted, a bit on the defensive, that "with the job and the kids, it's normal... sometimes. But I can still get it up!" In the end, I decided not to talk about it any more. But from that moment, I started to really go downhill. The shot of scotch I allowed myself after a stressful day at the office turned into four or five shots per evening. Sometimes I even drank at lunch. I slept badly, trying to figure out what had gone wrong, why I was being punished.

— I can understand. In your position, lots of men would've done worse!

— A little longer and I think I would've gone under. Then one day, on day 253, I decided to stop thinking about it. Like an amputee has to force himself to stop thinking about his lost leg. I hated my penis with an absorbing passion. I didn't talk to it any more, didn't even look at it. I gave it the silent treatment, like a kid. That lasted for two days. On the third day, I sunk really low, and phoned Eve for comfort. She was chilly at first, but I told her I really needed her, and used all my charm to convince her. I told her my problem still hadn't been solved but I needed a willing ear and a shoulder to cry on. She finally accepted. All that sincerity won her over...

I hadn't seen her since we'd broken up. I remembered her delicate contours with sadness — she was so beautiful, and all woman. I thought about how understanding she'd been. She'd really tried everything... I had been lucky to find a woman like her. But despite all her efforts, the sexier she was, the more stubborn my cock became. The more she tried to reassure me, the more I disappointed her. I owed her a lot, starting with a lot of respect and a big apology.

— Humility seems to work pretty well with women...

— This wasn't just humility... it was total despair! I rang her bell, feeling pretty anxious, and what a shock I had when she answered the door. She was wearing an old sweat-shirt covered with paint stains. Her hair was sloppily pinned up, with bits hanging in her face and eyes. She looked terrible! No makeup, holes in her socks, and that shapeless sweatshirt hiding her gorgeous curves... I was really worried and asked her what was wrong. But before she even answered, down in my pants I felt the first real stirring I'd felt in months. "I can't believe it!" I said to my-self. "What a scarecrow!" But it was true! I discreetly looked down at my own sweatsuit and couldn't believe my eyes! A hard on, so hard that it made a little tent in my pants! Eve followed my gaze and her eyes widened. She decided to let me in. She was worried what the neighbours would think. But I sensed she was sceptical. She was probably telling herself that at any moment, the "tent" would fall down, leaving me humiliated one more time. She led me in and went to the kitchen to get me a beer. It was then I saw, through a hole in her pants, that she was wearing the horrible pink underpants we always used to make fun of! They were baggy and had lost their elastic, and hung out the back of her pants. Seeing them, my hard on was back, half an inch longer than usual. What was going on? Was this what made me hard now? Everything was backwards...

Eve came back with the beer and looked at my crotch in disbelief. But all she did was smile, not wanting to add to my disappointment.

As for me, all I could think about was tearing those horrible clothes off her! Afraid of seeing my hopes fly away once again, I told her I'd had a solid erection for over five minutes. Wow! Another minute or two and I'd be leaping for joy! Eve pointed out that her clothes weren't exactly sexy... Maybe that was the explanation, I told her, then asked her what kind of bra she was wearing. She lifted her sweatshirt to reveal a dowdy beige bra that covered her breasts entirely. It was old and falling apart, with threads hanging off it. Nothing attractive — quite the opposite! But again my dick leapt up, and a little drop formed at the end, almost burning me. It had been such a long time...

Eve eyed me intently. She took off her sweatpants, displaying her pink underpants in all their ugly glory, then her sweatshirt. She stood before me, decked out in horrible underwear and socks with holes, and I just got harder. I was big and hard as a stallion. She pulled down my pants and sucked me. I kept waiting for the moment of defeat... but it didn't happen! She went to the sofa, beckoning to me, and pushed the crotch of her underpants aside without taking them off. I entered her in one stroke, harder than I'd ever been. Eve made love to me slowly, tenderly. I loved her with my whole cock, determined to make the pleasure last as long as possible.

When I finally came, it was with a flash of lucidity: "What horrible underwear!"

FOR A GOOD CAUSE

$\mathcal{T}$he door opened with a creak and my old friend Liza made her entrance. She looked at me from head to foot, flashed her famous smile, and sat down. She was obviously waiting for me to start talking. I knew we'd have plenty of time to talk about less important things later, so I got right to the heart of the matter. That's what she'd come for. I swallowed hard, collecting myself, then began.

— Remember how my mother used to say "Men will be your ruin, my girl"? Well, my dear, once again, years later, I have to admit she's right. You wouldn't believe what kind of mess I'm in. Me! A mature woman who's supposed to make the right decisions and be able to judge facts and consequences. But no! I've been had like a teenage girl, and even a teenager wouldn't have ended up in such a predicament...

— Start at the beginning. I'm not up to date with your life, you know...

— Of course, I'm sorry... My problems began just after I moved into my new place. Last year, remember? Before that I lived in an apartment building where I'd been happily living for years. And I'd never planned to leave there, either — twenty stories high with some really nice and obliging neighbours, Steve and Sylvie, who gave me the chance to indulge my exhibitionist tendencies.

— Well, well, well. How did this happen?

— It was all very innocent. I just hadn't bought drapes for the big windows in my bedroom. My lover at that time liked to watch me dance with all the lights on. To please him one night, I prepared a little demonstration of my skills, and then realized that my neighbours could watch us making love — and I'm pretty sure they took full advantage of it! The cross-shaped architecture was another wonderful thing about that building!

Anyway, this kind of performance was a source of pride for me, and I took pleasure in showing my neighbours what else I was capable of. It didn't take me long to realize they were looking at me every chance they got. That was a huge turn-on for me. Then there was Dave. A big muscular guy with a huge cock. I know you'd have liked him. I'd been seeing him for about a month, then his wife — of course I didn't know he was married! — came over and threatened me in very explicit terms. What a letdown. Dave was a fantastic lover and I was getting attached to him. I'm not all that sentimental, but I'd have liked to spend more time with him. True, he was a bit rough and his prick was really huge, but he was wonderful. I let him go with great regret, and tried to set my sights on the future. But his humiliated wife did her best to make life difficult for me... Then a friend of mine found the perfect solution. Do you remember Elaine?

— The real estate agent?

— Yes. It was pretty obvious I needed a change of scene, so she convinced me to buy a house. She quickly came up with something she knew I'd like. The house was a real find, and within my price range.

From the moment I moved, I found being a homeowner very pleasant. I missed my old neighbours, but I told myself something exciting would happen in my new environment so I wouldn't regret moving. Meanwhile, the only souvenir

I had of Dave was a thin leather belt that he'd left at my place by accident. He'd used it one night to whip me, tenderly. It was an intense and delicious memory, and I never hesitated to use the belt when I felt the need.

Then one day, a green van pulled up in front of the house and a young man rang my doorbell, offering to take care of my lawn. "It's not my lawn that needs taking care of!" I said to myself, looking at the splendid young guy. He looked so nice, I hired him on the spot.

As I watched him work in the hot July sun, I couldn't help noticing him glancing in my direction. He was cute as anything! He had a look of self-confidence, but I guessed it was a front because he blushed each time he looked at me. I asked him if he'd agree to come once a week, and offered to pay him in advance. He eagerly accepted, and once his work was done he came in for a few moments so I could pay him. After a few words of thanks and brief introductions, he left with a little wave.

— Oh, oh! When you say "young guy"...?

— Not even twenty! But let me continue!... During the heat wave, in the evenings, I acquired the habit of turning on the radio and slipping into the pool, naked as the day I was born. I had the pool built when I moved in. The water was perfect, just the right temperature for cooling down an overheated body. I paddled around a few moments, then let myself float on my back, admiring the starry sky. After a few minutes of this, my body drifted of its own accord to the powerful water jet from the filtration system.

The churning of the water was intense, and I let it massage my breasts, my belly... my inner thighs. My body warmly welcomed this unexpected caress. I spread my legs a moment and let the hot whirlpool massage me. Then, on impulse, I got out of the pool, wrapped myself in a towel, and went to get Dave's belt. As usual I got turned on just touching it. I slid it between my legs, down my back, my belly. Then I grabbed it at either end and slid it back and forth between my legs, letting the leather rub my swollen sex.

It was totally dark, so I could lie down on the chaise longue and finish with my hand what the belt had started. After a few minutes of this, I silently came, thinking of Dave, my old neighbours, and the young man who'd come over that afternoon...

Suddenly I heard the crackling of a branch. I snapped to attention and listened. There was soft laughter and murmuring whispers coming from the yard that backed onto mine. Had they seen me? Who were they? I was dying of curiosity. I wrapped myself in a towel and crept over to the neighbours' fence.

A couple was lying in the grass, kissing and laughing. They were obviously trying to be quiet, but without much success. I couldn't see their faces, just the outlines of their bodies. They seemed young, maybe even teenagers. The boy seemed to be making advances and the girl trying to stop him. You could tell from her stifled giggles that she was nervous. She allowed him to caress her young chest, though he wasn't very gentle. But then when he tried putting his hand inside her shorts, she jumped to her feet. All trace of laughter was gone, and she ran away crying: "Not that, Sean! You promised!"

Sean... was it the same Sean who had come to my house that afternoon? Probably. Poor guy! So cute but couldn't get what he wanted... I said to myself, "He should choose older, less uptight girlfriends!" I didn't want him to know I was there, so I crept back inside, poured myself a drink and sipped it in front of the television before falling asleep.

* * *

Liza was hanging on to my every word. She had even taken off her jacket and shoes to listen more closely. She knew me well enough to know I wouldn't keep her in suspense unless it was worth the wait.

I continued with pleasure.

— The next day was as hot as the day before. I didn't have the energy to get dressed, so I stayed in my bathing suit all day. I didn't do anything very strenuous, just lazed in the sun with a good book, taking an occasional dip in the pool, which had proved to be a worthwhile investment!

Later in the morning, I saw my backyard neighbour. It was the young man who'd come to take care of my lawn and had such an unpleasant setback the night before. He slaved away, ripping up weeds and trimming the hedge here and there. I suddenly felt sorry for him, seeing him so hot and sweaty. I went to the fence between our two properties and called to him, inviting him for a swim. He replied with a broad smile. As I walked away, I mused about how red his face had become when he accepted my invitation. Was it me having that effect on him, or was it the heat? "Maybe a bit of both," I decided.

He showed up in the late afternoon, carrying a towel and wearing a pair of baggy shorts. He greeted me politely, then hesitated. I motioned for him to go ahead, and watched him dive into the pool. He didn't have to be asked twice! He remained in the water for awhile, then got out. He was really adorable. Very tall, a bit on the thin side, but his muscles seemed firm and on their way to getting bigger. His skin was smooth and tanned a beautiful gold colour. His features were a bit feminine. He was going to be an incredible charmer when he grew up.

"How old is he, anyway?" I wondered. I tried guessing, but then decided just to ask. "Uh, nineteen," he answered, blushing again.

— The perfect age... A dream come true! Liza said, enchanted.

— Yes, he really was the boy of every girl's dreams... I offered him a beer. He hesitated a moment, then accepted gratefully. When I came back out of the house, he was sitting at the edge of his chair, his rumpled towel spread over his lap. I handed him the beer and took a long swallow from mine before jumping into the delicious water. Once I'd cooled off, I eagerly got out and sat down next to him with a smile of contentment. I asked him: "So are you still in school?"

Sean took awhile to answer. He was wearing sunglasses so I couldn't really see his eyes, but I guessed he was looking down my top. As if coming out of a fog, he rumpled the towel over his lap even more, and stammered: "Uh, no. Maybe I'll go back one day but for now I just want to work. My mom isn't too happy about it..."

"Do you have a girlfriend?" I asked him.

"I did until last night. Something happened and... she took it badly."

I decided not to pursue the subject. He wasn't about to confide in me, he barely knew me. But I was dying of curiosity.

"You'll meet someone else, a handsome guy like you..."

Sean blushed under his tan, but still managed to smile.

"Yeah, I know. And I'll have to get used to things ending

the same way each time. Maybe I'm too impatient, if you know what I mean..."

"I don't want to discourage you, but that doesn't necessarily get better with age..."

"And you, are you married?... Sorry, I shouldn't ask things like that..."

"That's all right, you can ask anything you want! No, I'm not married and I don't think I'll be getting married soon. Things are pretty quiet in that department these days."

"Yeah, I know what you mean."

After a few moments of silence and a few swallows of beer, Sean got up to leave, thanking me for everything. I watched him leave, and I called after him, "Any time, don't be shy!" I couldn't help admiring his young body, those long limbs that would fill out over the next few years. I made an effort to remember my boyfriends when I was his age. I suppressed a long shudder. Oh, if only I'd realized back then how lucky I was! Nothing was very complicated. It was a time of great discoveries, dizzy revelations, physical as well as emotional. The first caresses behind a bush. The first time you realize, as a woman, the near-limitless power you have over men. The dangers, the things you shouldn't do, classmates' gossip... Those were the days!...

Sean was probably at that time of his life, exploring a demanding and impetuous sexual nature. But judging from his remarks, he didn't seem to be meeting with much success. I thought maybe I could help him, give him a few pieces of advice. At nineteen, it was high time he learned! He was already missing out on the best things in life!

— You're telling me! Liza concurred. Considering the average length of a man's sex life, there's not a minute to lose!

— The next Friday was cooler than the days before. I

took advantage of it to take an evening walk around the neighbourhood. I savoured the quiet of the well-kept little streets, and the general air of serenity. I inhaled the light fragrance of the many flowers and trees, listening to the crickets and cicadas. When I turned the corner, I saw a van I recognized, full of gardening equipment. Inside was a boy, I guessed it was Sean, and a young woman. I ducked into the shadow of a tree.

I could see the silhouette of the couple, in sharp contrast with the light from the streetlights. They were kissing with charming abandon. Sean had his arms around the shoulders of the girl, who at least from that distance seemed quite willing. She took off her jacket. I smiled. Things were looking up for my little friend! I watched them in silence for a few minutes. Suddenly the girl pulled away, hurried into her jacket, and opened the car door, crying: "It's just our first date and you already want to take my clothes off! What's it going to be in a week? Well, you're never going to find out!"

On that note, she fled, looking more angry than hurt. I watched her go, then came out of hiding and went back to my nocturnal walk. I didn't want Sean to know I'd seen him lose face. I passed the van, which hadn't moved, hesitated a moment, then walked around to the door on the driver's side.

Sean was sitting behind the wheel smoking a cigarette, motionless. He didn't seem to understand what had just happened. Maybe he was totally discouraged. Seeing me, he gave a little wave. I spoke first.

"She didn't seem in a very good mood..."

"Oh! So what else is new..."

"You don't seem too perky either. Do you want to talk

For a Good Cause

about it? We could go for a beer at the corner..."

"Yeah, a beer would be good. Get in!"

I climbed into the old van and let myself to be driven to a little bar a couple of blocks away. Once we got there, we ordered a pitcher that he hastened to pay for, before I could protest. I tried to get him to talk. He explained that it was always the same: he'd meet a girl he liked and get her to go out with him, but then he ruined everything. "I always want to go too far, too fast! I don't do it on purpose, it's just..."

I tried to tell him it was that way for all boys his age, and suggested he go out with slightly older girls. He burst out: "But I'm too young for the girls I need! What do girls want? They show they like you, then you make a move and bang! They slam the door in your face!"

I tried to get him to admit that he was used to this sort of setback... It was then I learned that he'd never...

— Never...?

— Made love with a woman.

— You're kidding... at nineteen! What a miracle. Too gorgeous to be true. So how did you manage not to jump him then and there?

— Very funny... Yes, I was surprised, but I didn't let it show. He explained that until recently, he was too shy to go out with girls, and wanted to make up for lost time. He also knew the first time was the most wonderful, delicate and important...

I preferred to change the subject. I was afraid, as you say, that I might jump him. In truth, the more I thought about it, the more his confession was having an effect on me. He had never made love with a woman! I thought young people were so precocious these days... But there are exceptions to every rule. Still, I felt too generous of soul not to think seriously about what he'd told me. Maybe I should offer to initiate him into the joys of sex? After all, I was single, and it could be fun. There were advantages for us both! The idea was so interesting, it deserved serious consideration... but later, at home, when I could think clearly.

— But you finally gave in, didn't you?

— Patience!... So we talked about this and that for about three hours, then Sean took me home. As I left him, my mind was almost made up. But I didn't want to reveal my intentions just yet. I gave him a chaste little kiss on the cheek and got out of the van. Before leaving, he said he'd be at my place the next day, as planned.

That night I put Dave's belt aside and started thinking about the task ahead. What would be the best way to proceed? There was no doubt in my mind that he was attracted to me. I've never underestimated my own appeal and I wasn't about to begin. Nature's been kind to me and I've always worked to maintain my assets. Anyway, his attraction to me was quite obvious, judging from the towel on his lap the other day. What young man could resist the charms and desire of a woman like me? — so what if I'm thirtysomething!

— Not a lot of guys have resisted, at least not that I know of! my friend exclaimed.

— Well, there you go! And that wasn't going to change. I had a few choices. I could always lure him into the house on some pretext, like in a cheap porn film, then unveil my charms in all their dazzling splendour. Or I could be more subtle and let him guess my intentions. But that would take more time and it would be a shame for him to waste another minute. So I chose the first approach, the more direct one. Predictable, yes, but it had always worked and might be even more memorable for a young guy like Sean.

— And for you too, admit it!

— Yes, for me too. So I spent the whole morning working out the details. Lots of young people from my generation used to fantasize about older women. If this was Sean's case too, I'd give him a run for his money. I chose my silver bikini, which barely covered my ample breasts. I tousled my long blonde mane, put on perfume and my highest high-heeled sandals that made my legs look even longer. I put on light makeup, trying to look younger so as not to make him nervous. When I was finally ready, I sat down in my chaise longue, put on dark glasses, and became absorbed in reading my novel.

— The poor kid. You really went all out!

— Yes, and I could quickly see that my preparations were successful. Sean showed up a little before noon. When he saw me, he could barely swallow for a few long seconds. What a sight! I let him work, pretending to ignore him, making sure to leap into the pool from time to time. That way he could admire my almost naked body. From all appearances he was dazed, and his work showed it. When he finished the lawn, I asked him if he'd eaten. He seemed to appreciate my concern. I made him a sandwich and brought it out to him with a cold beer. Then he went back to work, just as distracted as before. From behind my glasses I could see he was looking at me every chance he got. My plan seemed to be working like a charm. When he finished shaping the hedges, I invited him to go for a dip, and he accepted with joy. He took off his jeans — he was wearing shorts underneath —, and leaped into the inviting water. I let him paddle around for awhile, then walked over to the pool myself with a slow and lazy stride. Sean gaped at me.

111

The poor boy looked like he didn't know what to think. I slowly climbed down the ladder, as if getting used to the water bit by bit. Once I was all the way in, I swam a few lengths before joining him at the side of the pool. Passing behind him, I casually let my breasts brush his tanned back and my thigh slide down his buttocks, as if by accident. He jumped as if he'd been stung, but stayed sitting in the same place. I left him there, swimming across the pool once more then getting out to lie down. I went into action: "I wanted to ask you..." I said, "There are some boxes in a closet I'd like moved into my room but they're too heavy for me. Could you give me a hand?"

I told myself if he hadn't caught on, he must be really slow. But to my great delight, he said he'd be happy to help. His face lit up. He furtively glanced between his legs. Apparently satisfied with the state of affairs, he got out of the pool, quickly dried himself off, and signaled that he was ready. "Poor sweetie, you don't know what you're getting into!" I said to myself with a smile.

— Yes, I can just imagine your face... I've seen how you look at times like that, just before you pounce on some poor defenseless victim!

— Defenseless, but not without resources! I took him into the room I was using as an office and pointed to a couple of big boxes on a shelf in the closet. He took one and waited for further instructions. Passing in front of him, I went to the staircase. I took the stairs slowly, so Sean's young eyes could get the best possible view of my hips. When we got upstairs, I walked to my room, feeling Sean's gaze on me and shivering with anticipation. I took a chair and put it in front of the open door of the closet, climbed up and made a space for the box. I turned to take it from the young man, making sure to lean over him so he got a good eyeful of my breasts. His Adam's apple slowly rose, as if it were about to strangle his already difficult breathing. Turning one last time to get rid of my burden, I arched my back, sticking out my buttocks which brushed his chin. It was then I delivered the *coup de grâce* by asking him to help me get down...

Leaning on his shoulders, I slid down along his body and found myself in his arms. The contact brought a pleasant rush of heat to my body. Seeing Sean's state of paralysis in this unforeseen situation, I took his hands and ran them down my body, then placed them on my impudent breasts. He was almost trembling, poor boy! I guided his fingers towards the fastener of my bathing suit, which was held together by just one little buckle, and had them perform the necessary gesture to undo it. My breasts were suddenly free. This time, I no longer had to guide his hands. He softly touched my pale flesh, barely brushing his hands over it. He seemed to be waiting for some sign from me, further proof that my advances were serious. I kissed him tenderly, tickling his hot mouth with my roving tongue. Then, just to make sure he had understood, I pulled down the tiny bottoms of my bathing suit and slid a thigh between his long legs.

— He never stood a chance! Liza exclaimed, feigning indignation.

— He certainly didn't! And his erection gave me the greatest pleasure. His surprise hadn't completely disabled him! I ordered him to get undressed immediately. He didn't move at first. I went to the bed and lay down in an inviting position. He finally made up his mind, and stripped his clothes off with wild gestures. Seeing his urgency, I went to

him and tried to reassure him, showing him that I wasn't
going to change my mind, that there was no hurry. He
stood in front of me, totally naked, and his erection was utterly satisfying. I forced myself to calm down. I reminded
myself he'd have a hard time holding back, seeing as it was
his first time. But I couldn't leave him standing there either! He looked so vulnerable and hesitant, not daring to
make a move, in case his beautiful dream vanished. I had
him come to the bed, taking his round little buttocks in my
hands and kissing his cock softly before taking it completely
into my mouth.

— Ah! the sweet little cheeks of a young man... what a
delicacy! My friend had a dreamy look in her eyes.

— But I didn't dare go at it too hard, I wanted to prolong
the episode as long as possible, though I knew it'd be short
despite all his best intentions. But he tasted good and my
mouth stopped obeying me, carrying on with the passionate
movements it was so used to and liked so much. I took him
deeper in my mouth, sucking harder as he went in and out,
overjoyed by how erect he was. After a few seconds, the in-
evitable happened. He flooded my mouth with his hot and
salty seed. His panting breaths made me look up. There was
a look of embarrassment on his face. I pulled him towards
me and tried to be comforting, assuring him that I was far
from finished. I kissed him again and had him lie down next
to me. I gently pushed him away so my hands would be free.
And then, my dear Liza, you would've been proud of me...

— What did you do this time?

— I gave him the most beautiful gift in the world... And
it'll last him a lifetime. I looked at him tenderly and murmured: "I'm going to give you a little lesson on female pleasure. So pay attention..."

Liza looked at me with deep respect. Once again I had impressed her, and surprised her with my ingenuity and savoir-faire.

— I ran my hands down my silky body, teasing each nipple to make it hard. I asked him very quietly, almost whispering, to caress them with his tongue, suck on them softly, very softly. Then I spread my thighs and freed my sex so I could caress myself. I interrupted Sean for a moment and asked him to watch carefully what my fingers were doing. He did what he was told, fascinated. He was a good student. His eyes were riveted to my hand, studying every touch, every movement. When my finger finally disappeared inside, he wanted to join in. I let him, asking him to be gentle for the moment. His hand did a wonderful imitation of what my fingers had taught him. He softly rubbed the sensitive flesh with a look of intense concentration on his face. Sensing he was ready for the next lesson, I showed him the little mound of flesh in the centre of my sex. "With the right touches here, you can make me cry out with pleasure!" I guided him there with all the necessary patience. "Yes, there... softly... Let your saliva run down, it's even better like that... That's it. Now go around it, softly, suck me a little, lick me all around. That's so good! Now put your finger inside. Gently! Go in and out slowly... faster... Oh, yes! Touch me now. Go back to what you were doing before, but faster. Not harder, just faster. Yes, like that... It feels so good...!"

Sean was great. He worked over me like a pro. I took full advantage of his caresses for as long as I could, attempting the impossible, trying to put off coming. But he applied himself so well that I couldn't hold back. My orgasm was unusually powerful. It seemed to go on forever. Sean watched me with a worried look on his face. I took a moment to catch my breath, then drew him towards me again, telling him how much I had liked what he'd done.

— Well, I certainly hope so! It's not fair! Do you think he'd like to practice with someone else, your Sean?

— Maybe. You'll have to ask him yourself... Anyway, I realized he had already recovered. His stiff cock was pressed against my sex, which was still pulsing with spasms...

— Another wonderful example of what a young body can offer!

— One among many! To reward him, I got him to lie on his back, kissed his soft face and adorable body. I didn't linger over his cock this time. I wanted to give him what he'd been waiting for...

I crouched down over him and had him penetrate me. He cried out a little and tried to move inside me. I held him back, satisfied just to lift myself a little so that nothing but the very tip of his cock was inside me. He seemed to understand what I wanted and let me lead the way. I slowly slid down on him, half an inch at a time, contracting the muscles of my vagina in a loving squeeze. I went a bit faster, giving him a foretaste of what he was waiting for, and he cried out again with a surprised look on his face. I massaged him this way for a few moments then got up. I asked him to kneel down in front of me. He did not resist. I turned my back to him and got down on my hands and knees, presenting my open pussy so he could enter me himself this time. Unable to wait a moment longer, he plunged into me hard, grabbing my hips, abandoning all reserve, thrusting with violence, pulling out at the very last moment to shower my buttocks with his sperm. He fell back on the pillows, eyes wide, as if he were in a state of shock. A smile slowly spread across his young face with its peach-fuzz.

Huddling against him, I asked if it had been the way he'd imagined. Amazed, he pulled me close and exclaimed: "A hundred times better!" His breathing slowed until finally he fell asleep.

* * *

Liza was green with envy. She tried to collect her thoughts and remember why she had come to see me. But first, she wanted to hear what happened next.

— That first time was a revelation for my young friend. But he couldn't believe what had happened. He seemed to think I'd push him away if he tried to get close to me again, and put an end to his education. He kept his distance for a few days. I started thinking that for him, our adventure had just been an excuse to get on with his own experiences. Maybe... But there was something that made me want to see him again, if only to confirm my skills as an instructor.

I met him on the street by accident, four days after our encounter. Seeing me, he blushed furiously, not quite knowing what attitude to take. I gave him my most ravishing smile and kissed him on the cheek, then asked him why he never came to see me. He told me he didn't want to impose. "You must have other boyfriends. I must've just been a one-time thing. Maybe you felt sorry for me or something?" I explained to him, for once and for all, that I had done it for just one reason — because I had wanted to. I insisted that our last meeting had been as good for me as it had been for him, and suggested he come back. I invited him to stop by a bit later that day and he joyfully agreed.

He showed up at my door in the early evening. I made hamburgers and we talked. The night was hot and as it grew dark, I suggested we take a dip. I took off my clothes in front of him and jumped into the pool. Sean came and joined me. I pressed myself against him, wrapping my legs around his waist. He was very hard. I let myself float on my back, my sex pressed against his. Then I swam to the water jet, and opened my thighs. Sean came to me and added to the massage with his well-trained hand. He hadn't forgotten any of what I had taught him!

He went around in front of me and penetrated me hard. We floated together gently, anchored to each other. I just had to hold onto the edge of the pool and let myself float on top of him, our bodies weightless. After a few moments, Sean pulled away and dragged me out of the pool. Lying on his side in the cool grass, he brought me towards him and entered me again. His movements were already more sure, more firm. He made love to me himself, like a big boy, with no interference from me. It was delicious! He was behind me, plunging into me, while his hand strayed over my wet vulva, looking for that most sensitive point. I helped him, and came with a sigh, which he took as a signal to come too. He stayed by my side a few moments, then we parted with a kiss, promising to get together again soon.

Sean had discovered an insatiable appetite. He came to my house at all hours of the day and night. I really liked him, so I always let him in. What's more, he seemed so eager to learn... Though admittedly, I didn't give him much choice. Each time had to be different from the time before. And these lessons became more productive with practice. Sean's stamina improved over the days. He managed to control his orgasm more and more, in order to satisfy me. I showed him new ways of making a woman come, giving him entire courses on anatomy and showing him the many possibilities of the common vibrator or any other object at hand. Once he even surprised me by jumping ahead of the night's lesson and taking an initiative that I welcomed with joy. He had been at my place awhile and we had shared a bottle of excellent wine that made us gently euphoric. We were naked, and Sean started to slowly massage my body. He started with my temples, making little circles around my hairline, then worked on my shoulders that were tense from working in the garden. Next he massaged my breasts with great appetite, licking and sucking with such application that I felt as if he'd known their secrets forever. Spreading my thighs, he first made me come with his hand then with the neck of the bottle that he inserted several times, watching for my reaction, observing in fascination as my sex welcomed it with pleasure. Later that night, I introduced him to the joys of a fur glove. I jerked him off very slowly, giving his member time to waken to the rhythm of my caresses, and marvel at the sensation of the fur on his delicate skin. It was beautiful to see his member grow erect so slowly! It grew bigger and bigger with each beat of his heart, and I took full advantage of every second.

Sean also proved to be a master in the art of tying my feet and wrists to my bed, and possessed me as if he'd been doing it all his life. After several first attempts, during which I showed the patience of an angel, he became an expert, knowing the exact amount of force I wanted him to restrain me with, and with how much ardour I wanted him to possess me. He penetrated me from the front, from behind, thrusting furiously and for longer and longer until I begged him to stop. As for me, to reward his many efforts, I showed him my whole repertoire. Slow dancing on top of furniture, the way I used to do for my former neighbours. An elaborate display in which I masturbated before a mirror, showing

my young lover the many possibilities of a candle. I unveiled the secrets of near-painful — but so pleasant! —
masturbation, and pseudo-forced sex. He found it all sublime. The first time I allowed him to take me by force, I had
to explain four times that it was what I really wanted. I
made him hit me, slap me, and penetrate me with so much
force that I had trouble walking for several days after.

Our affair went on for about three weeks — three weeks
of intense lovemaking, sometimes tender, sometimes violent. As I got to know him a little better, I prepared for the
moment when I'd have to tell him it couldn't last forever.
Eventually he would find a girl his own age that he'd like a
lot. He would have to be patient with her, and I taught him
that too. I explained that he always had to respect his
partner and never do anything to hurt or humiliate her, unless she asked him very clearly to do so, as I had done.

He listened religiously to all I had to say. I was happy to
see he was not at all in love with me. At first I'd been worried he would be. But he reassured me, saying he expected
nothing more than what I was giving him, knowing it
would end one day.

However, it ended much more suddenly than either of us
expected...

— With such a good thing going, why on earth end it?
Liza was perplexed.

— It wasn't my choice, believe me. And the reason I
asked you to come today will become obvious in a few minutes. One night — I didn't know it would be our last — we
had just finished the last of some chocolate mousse we'd
been enjoying after an afternoon of all kinds of acrobatics.
We were lying together completely naked on the living
room floor, looking at the coffee table almost affectionately.

The things we had just been doing would remain engraved in my mind for a long time. And I was amazed that it had not collapsed! It was heavenly! The room was such a mess, it looked like it'd been ransacked. Looking at it, we burst into uncontrollable laughter. At that moment, the doorbell started ringing insistently. I ran to get a dressing gown. When I opened the door, much to my surprise I found two policemen standing there, impeccably uniformed and looking sinister. They flashed their badges at me and announced:

"Miss Delaney, you are under arrest..."

"But what's going on?" It was then I saw Sean's mother. She pushed between the two policemen, planting herself in front of me, glaring at me with indignation, even hysteria.

"You should be ashamed of yourself! Doing this to my son, my little boy! I know what you've been up to, I know everything! You're nothing but a whore, picking on a seventeen year old boy for your filthy fun and games!"

So that's it. Sean lied to me. And since that fateful night, I've been waiting for the verdict. Do you think you can help me?

Of Satin and Lace

$\mathcal{I}$t was not until he got home that Matthew found the panties. He had gone to the corner laundromat to do his wash, as he did every Saturday morning. The place was deserted at that early morning hour, and he had taken advantage of the time to read a magazine he had just bought.

In short, it was a peaceful Saturday morning with the churning sound of the washing machine and the comforting roll of the dryer. However, when he got home and emptied the basket of clothes, which he had not taken time to fold, he saw them: tiny panties, pink satin trimmed with delicate lace. They seemed to be a small size. Unfortunately he was no expert at guessing the sizes of women's lingerie, but he could imagine the little buttocks that would fit inside the garment. And it was definitely not the sort of thing a mother would buy for her daughter...

He knew he should go back to the laundromat and leave the panties in some visible place so the owner could come back to get them. But they were such pretty panties... more likely to be carried off by some lonely guy. After thinking about it awhile, he decided to keep them — after all, he himself was lonely! Running his fingers over the soft material, he could not help but imagine all sorts of theories. Suddenly he had the image of a very pretty girl with long black hair tumbling down a slim, straight back. She was slipping the tiny panties up her long silky legs. This vision brought a flash of heat to his crotch. Matthew decided that

it was time to put an end to the "dry period" that had af-
flicted his personal life for too long, of which the panties
were a cheeky, stinging reminder.

Laying the panties on a chair, he changed his mind again.
He decided it would be better to take them back to the laundromat some morning the following week. In the mean-
time, he could leave them lying around wherever he
wanted! That is, until some prying female presence got the
brilliant idea of barging into his apartment!

However, the week went by and Matthew had still not
taken the panties back to the laundromat. He quickly realized how much he liked seeing them lying there on his
favourite chair. That way when he came into the house, he
had the illusion that someone was waiting for him.
Someone, maybe, had just taken them off, waiting for him
to return. What a pleasant fantasy!

The following Saturday, he totally forgot about taking the
panties back, he was so used to seeing them. They had become a familiar ornament in his otherwise spartan apartment, representing a hope that he never dared admit to
himself. It was not until he was putting his clothes in the
washing machine that he remembered. "Too late now. If I
see a woman who looks like she's searching for something,
I'll know what to do..."

He took his time that morning. It was not very likely that
the lady in question would show up, but he lingered for
awhile, just in case. He had nothing planned for the moment. The people he knew found him a little strange for
doing his laundry so early on Saturday morning, when most
people were sleeping in! Matthew had always been an early
riser. In fact, he had an unusually disciplined routine, at
least his colleagues thought so. He had no taste for bars

with pounding music where everyone paraded around in front of each other, hoping not to spend the night alone. Not that his nights were so full, far from it! He was in his fourteenth month of abstinence. No need to add that he wasn't about to shout this out from the rooftops...

His last affair had been a disaster. He'd had the unfortunate idea of getting a bit too interested in one of his clients, and it had backfired. She had waited two months before telling him she was married. "I'm still very much in love with my husband!" she had added. Ah... Maybe he was too idealistic, but to him she had not acted much like a woman in love with her husband. Anyway, that was all over. As for the others, he was too shy. And that was his biggest problem. His old friend Jane had even given him "courses" in how to approach women, much to her amusement.

Jane and him had spent their childhood and teenage years side by side — almost their entire lives. Matthew had taught her to play hockey and baseball, and she tried to return the favour by introducing him to single women. The results were always a disaster. The women were usually very nice, but there was always something not quite right. He could not bear for them to have expectations of him. The very fact of going out to dinner with someone who wanted a steady relationship made him so uncomfortable that he didn't know what to do. He felt cornered, as if he was supposed to behave in a way that was not natural for him. All those things you had to say and do were way too complicated! He had tried explaining that to Jane, but she was stubborn.

However, her hockey was improving like wildfire. Not bad, for a girl! He had trouble seeing her as anything else but a sort of tomboy, the way she was as a little girl and teenager. She was quite pretty, but her athletic skills took away her femininity. Anyway, he had never really paid attention to her charms, preferring to tell her his impressions of her various boyfriends. He loved her as a brother would. If only he could meet a girl like her! Well, almost like her...

This is what he was thinking about when the dryer stopped. He hurriedly threw his clothes into his basket and went home. His recent reflections had made his heart a little heavy. When he got home, he changed to go play baseball. Jane was supposed to arrive any minute.

* * *

She brought him back home at two in the afternoon. They were both starved after so much fresh air and exercise. He suggested making a quick lunch and going to eat in the park.

— I'll fold your laundry while you make something to feed me with.

— No, leave it... I'll do it when I get back!

— I've seen all your underpants and socks before, you know!

All that was left was to find something to drink. He was taking out a bottle of apple juice when he sensed a presence behind him. Jane was standing at the kitchen door with a superb pink satin bra hanging from the end of her finger. She was looking at it ironically.

— Are you hiding something from me?

— No! Where did you find that?

— In your laundry basket, little sneak! Come on, tell me! You're not going to start hiding your affairs from me, they're way too rare!

— But I swear... Wait, show me.

He took the bra and examined it from all angles.

— Stop playing dumb. Whose is it?

— Just be patient!

He went to the chair to get the famous panties, then re-membered he had put them somewhere else a few days be-fore. He came back and quickly realized they matched the bra.

— This is a bit much.

— If you're not going to tell me what's really going on, just invent something...

— Last Saturday, when I got home from the laundromat, I found this in my stuff. I was going to bring it back this morning but I forgot. And now, this!

— Sure, sure, she said sceptically.

— I swear! It's pretty incredible that I've ended up with both. It's a pretty strong coincidence!

— It sure is. Since you say it's a coincidence...

That is where the discussion ended. He was not going to bend over backwards to make her believe him. She could think what she wanted. And he was not going to admit to her that he had chosen to keep the panties. The decision had been made without him really noticing.

The determining incident had occurred on Wednesday or Thursday, he did not remember. He was watching televi-sion, as on any normal day, when his hand strayed to the satin panties. He imagined what he would do if the beau-tiful dark-haired woman of his dreams, owner of the panties, arrived at his door to claim them.

Little by little, the story became more elaborate. The stranger was not satisfied with just taking back her property and leaving, far from it! Without a word and to the rhythm of some inaudible music, she took off her clothes in front of him with precise and decisive gestures, charged with sensuality. Wearing only a bra, she put on the pretty panties, looking at Matthew with an inviting smile. But she didn't stop there! Seizing the lacy bit of clothing, she pulled it up over her round hips, her slim fingers sliding beneath the soft fabric, moving lower and lower. He was hypnotized by the long fingernails disappearing into the black bush that he had noticed earlier, guessing at her movements over her damp flesh. Finally, so he could fully admire the show, the beauty spread her legs and, pushing her panties aside, exposed her glistening sex whose sweet juices Matthew could clearly smell. Then with a skillful finger, she traced the contours of her full lips, applying a firm pressure before slipping inside the silky folds.

That was when Matthew had undone his pants, letting them fall around his ankles. He picked up the provocative panties, brushing their silky softness over his belly and thighs, still watching his seductress in the throes of pleasure. Without realizing it, he had started stroking himself, and kept on going until the panties were soaked and he emerged from his daydream, panting and more frustrated than ever.

After that, there was no question of him getting rid of the panties. He washed them carefully, almost lovingly. Their place of honour moved from his favourite chair to his sheets. They were his little secret. And now there was the bra, too...

Jane was still convinced that he was involved in some new affair that his legendary shyness prevented him from talking about. She twirled through the apartment, holding the bra out at arm's length with a jeering smile on her face.

— So are we eating, or what?

* * *

That evening, Matthew decided not to join Jane and the other guys on the hockey team who were going out dancing after the game. It was already late and he had drunk his Saturday night quota of beer. Obviously, Jane joked that he had a secret rendezvous and did not want to share the juicy details with his friends... The others fired questions at him until he finally got away, annoyed with Jane but not tired enough to go to bed right away. He turned on the radio and started reading his magazine.

He flopped down on the sofa and felt something underneath him. He reached under his buttocks and found the magnificent bra. In the state he was in, that was all he needed. He held it out delicately in front of him, trying to imagine the size and shape of the breasts that would comfortably fit inside it. He envisaged them as quite small but firm, with nipples the colour of milk chocolate stretching the fine material. He went to get the panties and, putting them on the sofa next to the bra, tried to imagine the body of the woman whom the silky ensemble would suit.

She was slim, quite petite, with subtle rather than pronounced curves. Oh, he did know her a little, after all! At any rate, her image was becoming clearer. She was the type to wear very elegant, feminine clothes, and high heels that would make her seem taller. She usually wore her hair up in a loose chignon, which it would give him the greatest pleasure to undo, freeing her long black locks.

She appeared before him again, teasing him, her deft fingers hovering over the buttons of her dress. Was she going to make up her mind or not? All of a sudden, *voilà!*... She unveiled her throat, then her chest in the pink brassiere whose colour contrasted with her mat complexion. The close-fitting dress slipped down slowly, until her flat stomach was exposed down to the fine lace trimming the edges of the tiny panties.

She had slipped on long fine stockings that she did not take off right away. For awhile now, Matthew had been stroking his cock, which was standing at attention and admiring the show. His movements became increasingly insistent. The young woman pinched each breast through the thin fabric, then freed them, offering them up to Matthew's hands and lips. He felt her flesh, firm and soft, just as he had imagined. He kissed her breasts, then avidly licked and sucked the erect nipples. The long hair tumbled down over the admirable chest, giving the woman an even more unreal and diaphanous look. She was with him on the sofa now, her slim legs on either side of him. He wanted to caress the fine waist, the small buttocks, but she pulled away and returned to her previous position. Turning, she let her magnificent hair fall down her back so Matthew could admire the other side of her body, her pretty hands wandering over her inviting buttocks. Facing him again, she got down on her hands and knees and moved slowly towards him with a feline stance. He tried to record each detail in his memory: pink panties and bra, silk stockings and high heels, spectacular hair, ravishing smile... until she buried her head between his legs, letting her pale full lips take over from the man's too-familiar hand. She nibbled the hardened cock then curled her tongue around it, before sucking it all the way into her mouth. She sucked more vigorously and quickly. Then she stopped suddenly, taking a moment to caress him with her hand. When Matthew had recovered some control, she started her relentless sucking again with even more force. She played this little game a few times, bringing Matthew to the brink of ecstasy then calming him down again so as better to torture him. He tried to last as long as he could, then finally closed his eyes and let himself go in her welcoming mouth. Refusing to rouse himself, Matthew fell asleep on the sofa, a milky little puddle on his stomach.

* * *

After this evening, stranger and stranger things started to happen. First of all, Matthew started getting hard-ons at any time of day. The mere thought of the satin bra and panties and — presto! he would feel like a stallion ready to jump any mare in sight. This phase lasted two weeks. If he did not soon meet someone and release some of his tension, he was going to explode. He masturbated almost every day... was he going through second adolescence? Worse, he seemed totally unable to control himself. In the shower, in the morning, before going to sleep at night... sometimes even in broad daylight, he would sneak off to the bathroom to quickly relieve his pent-up lust.

Another unusual event: one evening, while sipping a beer with his friends, he went off on his own to talk to a girl sitting alone at the bar. In his own defence, it must be said that he'd had a few beers too many, and the prospect of going home alone depressed him beyond reason. Thus, he went into action, and it worked! After several hours of quite pleasant conversation, she invited him home with her. She was tall and blonde, not particularly pretty, but Matthew made an exception, just this once. He needed a woman, there and then. So what if she was not the goddess of his dreams! Maybe she would make up for it in other ways. She gave him a beer, as he'd hoped, kissed him and let her hand go straight where it wanted. And she was not disappointed! The effect was immediate. Like a spring, he got so hard it was very uncomfortable. She encouraged him to get undressed and did the same in front of him, then asked him to come into her bedroom.

Matthew did not need to be asked a second time. At last, a change from his calloused hand! She sucked him briefly, but didn't seem to like it too much. Maybe she wanted to do something else? She got on top of him and slid him into her. In a single night, Matthew would make love in more positions than in his entire life. She had incredible imagination and flexibility! The girl also seemed just as sex-starved as him, and they went at it wildly, making each other come over and over until they fell asleep in total exhaustion.

When Matthew woke up, he did not know where he was and had a terrible headache. The pain got considerably worse when he saw the girl lying asleep in bed next to him. His first reflex was to get up and get dressed as fast as he could. What had happened? Was he so desperate that he'd picked this girl up and gone home with her? Scenes from the night before came back. She wasn't so bad, after all. But still! Did she spend each weekend night picking up guys?

Matthew shuddered. He was ready to leave. What was he supposed to do? Leave his phone number somewhere? But he was not sure he wanted to see her again. Still, he couldn't just leave like a burglar after the night they'd just spent together... Suddenly on a little table he saw what looked like a phone bill, with a name, an address, a number that he supposed were hers. He scribbled them down on a note pad, then put the piece of paper in his pocket. He left her a short note: "Sorry, I had to go early. Thanks for the great night. I'll call you." "You prick!", he said to himself.

"You could at least wake her up!" But he could also *not* wake her up, and that is what he finally did. It was Saturday, he had a lot to do, and frankly, he did not have the strength to lie out loud. He left the apartment like a coward, trying to convince himself that she had probably expected this sort of behaviour from him.

He was running late in his Saturday washing schedule, but still he stopped home and took a quick shower, then gathered his clothes and went to the laundromat.

* * *

He headed straight for "his" washing machines. Since it was still early for the average mortal, most of them were not in use and the place was fairly quiet. He was just about to put his things inside one of the washers when he saw some-thing inside, way at the back. He took it out and saw it was a silk stocking, like his imaginary lover was wearing on her last visit. He rolled it in a ball and stuck it in his jeans pocket. What luck! At this rate, he would soon have an en-tire woman's wardrobe! When his clothes were ready for the dryer, he put the stocking in the pile. When the clothes were dry, he would take it home with him.

When he got back to his apartment, he reached in his laundry basket and took out the stocking. Very soft, black, without any runs that he could see. He let it glide between his fingers, and almost immediately felt his cock grow painfully hard. He put the new item with the two others and allowed himself to daydream again. Would Sandy, the girl he had spent the night with, be able to wear this pretty underwear? Maybe he could ask her to put them on, just to see. He found it a bit strange to be masturbating while thinking of a girl who perhaps did not even exist, though his little fantasy was not harming anyone. The only risk of getting Sandy to wear the clothes was that it might destroy his image of the unreal woman who haunted his imagination. But he was ready to take that risk.

He spent that evening and those that followed wondering whether to call Sandy. But each time he went to dial her number, he could not help seeing her face and comparing it with the face of his mythical woman. Then he would change his mind. It was not until the following Saturday, when he found the other silk stocking in the dryer, that he started asking himself if this could really be an accident.

Who could be playing this little game with him? But he banished the ridiculous thought from his mind. This sort of thing did not happen to him. And it could not be anyone he knew, the only girl he was close to was Jane. And she wasn't really a girl... anyway, not in the sense of a potential lover. The day Jane would wear clothes like that was the day hell would freeze over! Maybe she was playing a joke on him? No, she wouldn't go that far! Still, he would try talking to her about it, just to see.

Matthew had a sudden inspiration. What if he went to the laundromat early? Maybe he would meet that absent-minded, mysterious woman who lost a new item of clothing each week! He would put his plan into practice the next weekend.

* * *

The following Saturday, as planned, Matthew went to the laundromat a full hour earlier than usual. He even had to set his alarm clock. He was an early bird, but not to that degree! The mystery was too great, he wanted to clear it up. But the only people there when he arrived were a fat bearded man with his young son, and an older woman in her late fifties or early sixties. "If that's her, I'm done for! I don't even want to think about it!" Judging from the very masculine clothes that the bearded man was washing, it was clear he had nothing to do with the whole saga. Still, Matthew went around to the washers and dryers, looking for a clue. There was nothing at the moment, so he went ahead with his weekly task, planning to observe the comings and goings of the other customers, and thinking about the drama of the night before.

He had called Sandy during the day, and she had seemed very happy to hear from him. They made a date to meet at her place that evening. On a sudden impulse, he had brought the clothes, though not quite knowing how to ask her to put them on. He had thought about it for awhile but felt it was a delicate request, seeing as it was just their second meeting. However, the temptation was too great. He had to try.

As he had hoped, she welcomed him with open arms. She was impatient and took him straight to the bedroom. Seeing his look of indecision, she thought he did not want her. For a moment, he beat around the bush, thinking of how to word his request. Finally he took the clothes out of the bag he had brought and showed them to her. She looked at them closely, then her eyes narrowed. Her whole face contorted with anger.

— What are those, your ex's clothes? Are you sick or what? I thought we were getting along fine just the two of us! Get out!

— Calm down! These aren't my ex's clothes! I'll explain later... But if you don't want to put them on, that's okay. Just forget it!

Matthew started to be more coaxing. He assured her the

clothes did not belong to another woman, he just wanted to
see her wear them because they were so pretty. She came
around after awhile and picked up the garments to get a
closer look. She seemed to appreciate their quality and softness. After a few moments' hesitation, she went into the
bathroom and came out wearing them. Matthew tried to
conceal his disappointment. What a disaster! The bra was
too tight and made her breasts bulge out unbecomingly.
The panties were too small as well, and her broad hips
spilled out over the elastic. It was just the opposite of what
Matthew had hoped. He was disappointed. Suddenly all he
could think of was leaving, but he had to get the clothes
back first...

— Thanks, Sandy. I just wanted to see if they fit you...

— You wanted to give them to me? How sweet of you!
Come here so I can thank you properly...

He went to her, but was disturbed by the sight of this girl
disfiguring the clothes that had brought him so much pleasure. He tried as nicely as possible to get her to take them
off, but the effect was ruined by his look of ill humour.
Seeing that he was no longer smiling, Sandy went back into
the bathroom then came out again in a dressing gown and
handed him the underwear, asking him to come to bed.
"What am I doing here? This girl does nothing for me!" he
thought. It was like a revelation. Ashamed of what he was
about to do, but resigned to his lack of desire, he said:

— Listen, Sandy, I've got to go... We'll... we'll save it for
next time, okay?

— What do you mean, you have to go? I was right, you're
a sicko! Get out, and don't bother calling me again!

— Well, okay, bye...

And that is how it ended. Matthew felt terrible... he had

behaved like a total jerk. What was with him these days? And anyway, how had he ended up in bed with this girl in the first place? Maybe his sexual "fast" had driven him a bit crazy. The very idea of asking Sandy to put on the underwear had been a serious mistake. She had spoiled the charm. He realized he knew nothing about women's sizes. The clothes had looked terrible on her! The mysterious stranger had to be much slimmer than Sandy, who had nonetheless seemed pretty slender to him. To his great astonishment, he started examining each girl he met on the street, trying to guess if by some chance she could wear the pretty underwear.

Time passed, his wash was done, and no possible suspect had come into the laundromat. He took care this time to fold his clothing before he left. Finding no items that did not belong to him, he felt a certain disappointment, and resigned himself to the idea of waiting another week before finding another clue.

He spent the week calling himself an idiot with a one-track mind. But he could not shake his obsession. He feared he was sinking into despair when he realized he was looking at Jane in the same way he was looking at other women.

They were all at the corner bar and Jane had showed up a little earlier, looking gloomy. She was standing and talking animatedly with Mark. Matthew did not listen to what they were saying. He had just realized how petite Jane was. Probably petite enough to... He chuckled to himself at the idea of seeing her dressed like that.

As for Jane, she seemed to be in a foul mood. He overheard a bit of the conversation.

"You men are so blind! It's like we have to throw ourselves at your feet and yell at the top of our lungs for you to notice us! It's really discouraging... And you probably wonder what we're yelling about!"

Matthew could not help but smile. If a woman wanted to be noticed by him, she did not have to do much! Poor Jane, still having trouble with men... she never chose the right ones! They drank a few more beers. Jane stopped talking about her obvious disappointment. The next day was Friday, and a holiday. They made a date to meet at the park in the morning to kick a ball around.

The game went as usual, an indescribable combination of seriousness and wild laughter. Matthew thought with a sort of jolt that it was Jane who made their times together so funny. Her bad mood of the night before seemed to have disappeared. Matthew invited her to his place for lunch. She accepted on the condition that he let her take a shower in his bachelor's lair, unkindly adding that the shower had not seen a woman's body for so long it would probably be shocked!

They ate quickly and Jane tried to find out if Matthew had "found" other clues from the mysterious stranger. He hid the stocking and the fact that he still had the adorable undergarments in his possession. What would she think of him? She obviously did not believe him, and would gleefully and openly make fun of him. She had not said anything about Sandy, no doubt feeling it was a delicate subject.

She helped Matthew clear the dishes away and went to shower. She had only been in the shower a couple of minutes when Matthew decided to go to the store to buy a few beers. He opened the bathroom door and asked Jane if she wanted anything. She yelled back that a cold beer would be good. He went to close the door again, but it was jammed...

He bent down to pick up the obstacle and saw a very pretty black bra made of satin and lace... He would never have believed she wore this kind of thing. Seeing it, he started getting an erection. He quickly kicked it aside in embarrassment, and closed the door.

Strange thoughts assailed him during his errand. Had Jane always worn underwear like that? To play ball? Did he know her so little? Suddenly uncomfortable, he hurried to buy the beer and return home. He hoped she would be finished her shower and dressed by the time he got back. He did not at all like the effect the black bra had had on him. He had just realized that Jane was a woman. Of course, he had always known, but had never really seen her that way. She had always been just one of the boys for him. And all of a sudden she had shown him, without even knowing it, that she was no more a man than he was a woman... What a shock!

When he got home, Jane was out of the shower and drying her hair. He was so uncomfortable that he told her he had to go out and do more errands. She did not seem to mind, and left without asking any questions.

* * *

Matthew had decided to stop looking for the mysterious stranger. There was no point in finding out who she was anyway. No doubt it was just an accident and he happened to be the lucky one. And if it was more than a coincidence, the woman in question should just be more direct. He was not going to play that game any more.

The next Saturday he went back to the laundromat, at the same time as on any Saturday morning. He did not look in the machines to see if anyone had left a piece of underwear. He was too preoccupied by the previous day's incident and worried about the fact that he could no longer see his friend Jane in the same light.

In fact, he was so absentminded that he did not see the new bra and panties until he got home. What a shock! He could have sworn it was the same bra that had blocked his bathroom door the day before. A pretty black bra made of satin and lace, with matching panties.

He felt his knees grow weak. He ran into the bedroom, compared the two sets of underwear and realized they were the same size. The size that Jane must wear! This revelation made him blush. Before he could do anything about it, the image of the beautiful stranger came back, but this time with Jane's features. Matthew felt ashamed at this fantasy and overwhelmed with confusion. He could not start desiring Jane, not after all this time! Not her! But the mere thought of his long-time friend wearing such sexy underwear made him go hard as a rock.

He tried forcing himself to think about something less exciting. What was he going to do? Lose a good friend overnight, just because his stupid brain would not let go of these disturbing images? Matthew had to face it: disturbing or not, they had a powerful effect on his crotch.

He felt panicky. Out of respect for his friend, he decided to tell her everything, and emphasize that it was driving him out of his mind. He seized the phone and mechanically dialed her number.

— Jane! I've got to see you right away!

— What's wrong? You sound all upset!

— Do you want to come here or should I go to your place?

— I'll be waiting for you.

Matthew ran the few blocks to Jane's in an altered state. He moved with a firm step, but had no idea how he was going to tell her what was bothering him. What would he do when he arrived at her apartment?

All he'd manage to do was make a complete fool of himself, but there was no turning back.

Why hadn't he waited for her to come out of the shower? Did he unconsciously know what was awaiting him? Hadn't he always known she was beautiful and available? Was it his unusual sexual appetite in the past weeks that had made him react in this way to an incident that was basically quite harmless? Or maybe she had planned it all...

Those were the thoughts he was mulling over when he rang her doorbell. After letting him in, she asked him why he was so upset.

— Jane, I don't quite know how to tell you, but something really embarrassing is going on. It started a few weeks ago. You know, the time I found the panties in my laundry...

— Yes, and then the bra...

— You still don't believe me, do you?

— Well... okay, if you insist. You look really freaked out...

— So anyway, yesterday when you were at my place and I asked you if you wanted something from the store, I saw your bra on the floor, and...

— And what?

— I never realized you wore things like that. And since then, I haven't stopped thinking about... about...

— About what, Matthew? Is it possible you're looking at me in another way?

— Exactly! And it bothers me... I've always loved you like a sister, but now I'm getting all sorts of crazy ideas...! I don't know what to do! You're going to hate me, and I can understand why!

— Hate you? Matthew, I could never hate you!

With that, she opened her dressing gown, revealing her throat, her small breasts enclosed in a magnificent pink bra whose colour contrasted with her mat complexion. She let the dressing gown slide down her body. Her flat belly was exposed down to the fine lace trim of the tiny panties.

The scene was so close to his fantasy that Matthew forgot all reserve and lunged at her. She smelled good and was so beautiful! He was stunned, hardly daring to touch her very soft skin. Jane took him in her arms and led him to her bedroom. Looking him deep in the eyes, she slowly undressed him, patiently undoing each button of his shirt, unzipping his pants with an almost solemn look on her face. Kneeling down in front of him, she covered his belly with soft kisses, letting her tongue wander over his swollen sex. Enclosed in her hot mouth, Matthew let out a deep sigh, allowing her to continue her ardent caress for a few moments longer before drawing her towards him. He held her against his chest, his fingers tangling in her silky hair, and finally kissed her. In his kiss were all the feelings he had for her, welling up all at once and making him dizzy. His last clear thought was that it was her, Jane, who had set everything up to lure him to her. And she had succeeded...

The two lovers were so close, they felt they had been making love together their whole lives, yet without becoming any less passionate. Their gestures were tender, full of love and affection. In a sweet dance of lust they moved together, covering each other with kisses and stroking each other with increasing urgency. Matthew relived every intense second of his recent fantasies, but this time with a real live woman! He could finally touch her, feel the texture of her skin, her supple legs, her round breasts. Their bodies twined around each other in the most natural way. Matthew tried to delay the ultimate moment when he would finally plunge into the companion he knew so well without ever having truly savoured her. But as their kisses and desire grew more ardent, they could wait no longer, and Matthew slid inside her. They fell into rhythm with each other, rocked by the movement of their hips, exploring each other's bodies with delight, curiosity and contentment. They seemed made for each other, Jane's hot sex perfectly gripping Matthew's impetuous member, now thrusting without restraint. He stopped a moment and knelt down behind her, lifting her close then plunging back into the heat of her prone body. His hands could not stop exploring her skin, lingering on her throat, nipping her graceful neck. His hand reached down and found her trembling lips, spread them and massaged them, revelling in the young woman's eloquent sighs. Matthew's pleasure grew more intense with every breath, and finally he came inside her in a great liberating wave. For long minutes after, he could feel the tremours of his companion's body. They fell asleep happy, any worries about the sudden change in their relationship far from their minds.

The following Saturday, light of heart, Matthew went off to do his laundry at the usual hour. He and Jane had scarcely been apart a minute since the night they had finally come together. He now realized how much he had always desired her. She fulfilled him in every way, and each moment away from her was painful. He spent his time at the laundromat thinking about the last few days, a smile of bliss on his lips. After the drying cycle was over, Matthew piled up his clothes and could not repress a mischievous smile when he saw a pair of pretty panties tumble out of the machine. He realized at this moment that neither he nor Jane had discussed the technique she had used so skillfully to seduce him. He was surprised that she had not yet given it up — obviously she had not. She'd really pulled one over on him! If it had not been for her and her adorable little game, they might not be having such a wonderful time together! How happy he was she had made the first moves!

He picked up the panties and put them in the basket with his other clothes. At that moment an older woman appeared, the one he had seen the day he had come a bit early, hoping to catch the trickster in the act. She seemed preoccupied, slowly walking around the room, examining every machine. After a few minutes of careful searching, she turned to Matthew with obvious embarrassment.

— Excuse me, young man, I don't suppose you happened to find something in the dryer? I'm so absentminded, I've been forgetting things for weeks when I come do my wash. I've lost all my nicest underwear, and my husband is starting to wonder...

DOUBLE OR NOTHING

$\mathcal{I}$ don't think I'll ever forget that eventful autumn. As the leaves on the trees changed colour and we, poor humans, braced ourselves for another few months of winter misery, my life was falling to pieces. In a single month — though it was a lovely September — my boyfriend left me, I lost my job, and almost got thrown out of my apartment for not paying the rent, which had, until then, been the responsibility of the said boyfriend.

After a long period of feeling sorry for myself, I had to face facts: I'd been asking for it! The whole tailspin started when Jerome left me, and for that, I had only myself to blame.

The problem began with a little party we threw to celebrate my birthday last January. I looked at my friends gathered together, realizing how lucky I was for such a show of friendship from so many people I liked and respected. But I suddenly understood that something was missing, some little thing that would make my life complete. And this little thing could be summed up in one word: "posterity". After I departed from this life, nothing would remain to continue my memory. Nothing tangible, anyway. After that moment, I could just think of one thing: having a baby. Of course, I'd thought of it before, I'd wanted to have a family for as long as I could remember. But I kept putting it off, again and again. "When I'm in better shape financially", I told myself. "When I've found a man I want to spend the rest of my life with", or "When I've fulfilled my career goals". When, when, when...

Analyzing my life that evening, several things became clear. First, I was living with Jerome, whom I loved enough to imagine as the father of my children. We didn't have a lot of money, but after all, wasn't love what counted, what a child needed most? As for my career, I had to admit, it wasn't turning out the way I'd hoped, and I seemed to be getting farther from fulfilling my goals, not closer. So what was holding me back from having a baby? The answer to all these questions was, obviously, "Nothing!" When I realized that, the idea of conceiving a child became a total obsession, despite my companion's lack of enthusiasm about my new "resolution". But I did not consider his attitude an obstacle. I'm a stubborn woman, and was sure that once he was confronted with a *fait accompli*, Jerome would jump for joy and welcome the little jewel with open arms. I was equally convinced that all I had to do for that miracle to happen was put away my contraceptives. To put my conscience at rest, I tried for several days, even weeks, to convince Jerome of the benefits of my plan. But this was no more than a simple formality. After persevering for awhile, I concluded that my happiness would be his happiness. I put an end to my attempts to persuade him and simply went into action. I stopped bothering him about it. I stopped talking about babies, stopped sighing as if my heart was broken when I saw an infant on television or in the street. In short, I pretended not to be thinking about it any more. What Jerome didn't know is that I'd also thrown my diaphragm away, saving only the case, which I left lying around each time we made love. If I conceived, I could always feign innocence and refer to it as an "accident", flatter him and tell him he must have dynamite sperm to get past that thick latex barrier...

To ensure the desired result, I had taken care to find out about the process. I knew which times of the month were useless and which times my plan was most likely to succeed. Maybe Jerome found me unusually forthcoming on those days I waited in bed for him to get back from work, wearing my skimpiest lingerie and striking the most enticing poses. But he never seemed to wonder about it, preferring to think it was plain desire, fired by his incomparable sexual prowess. Of course I let him believe what he wanted while trying not to be too obvious, because men are sometimes less stupid than they seem!

But anyway... eight months passed, and still nothing had happened. I started to get discouraged, and one day I was struck with a terrible doubt. It wasn't that easy after all — was something going wrong inside my body? I swept these unpleasant thoughts from my mind and tried to pull myself together. I took the initiative once again, taking advantage of the fact that we both had a week's holiday coming up, at exactly the right time. We were going to a charming little country inn where we could "give free rein to our passion". Jerome pointed out that our passion was already pretty un-reined as of late. But I told him: "You drive me wild! If you think I'm hot now, think how we'd be with a whole week to live out our fantasies!" He couldn't resist. On the tenth day of my cycle, we left for the country. I was already overjoyed by the idea of my baby being conceived in such an en-chanting setting.

For the whole week, I gave him no peace. I left nothing to luck or accident. True, I'd read someplace that you got the best results when you let a day go by between each relation so the man could "recover his strength", but I considered this detail totally unimportant. I used my imagination, seducing him in a different way each time to take full advantage of his precious juices. I transformed from courtesan to frightened virgin, from brazen whore to curious young girl, and he savoured each character with increasing vigour. I was in heaven! In seven days, we had made love at least eleven times, and I told myself that if it didn't succeed, it wasn't because we hadn't tried! But I didn't have the time or opportunity to elaborate on this theory because at the end of the month, Jerome finally figured out what was going on.

When my period arrived two weeks after our little adventure, I didn't have the strength or the desire to hide my disappointment. The first two days, I was in a foul mood, swamped in dark thoughts — this often happens in such cases —, and refused to get out of bed, moping around in a gloomy slump. On the third day, his patience worn out, contaminated by my bad mood, Jerome started a major housecleaning to calm his nerves. He cast me disapproving glances from time to time as I sat watching TV, stuffing myself with ice cream. Half an hour later, a livid Jerome snapped off the television and planted himself in front of me, flailing the diaphragm case like a lethal weapon.

— What's this doing in the bathroom, empty?
— What do you mean? It can't be empty...
— Caroline, what kind of game are you playing?

Oh-oh! He'd caught on... I didn't have the energy to deny anything, feeling it was a losing battle. A terrible quarrel followed. He called me every name under the sun, accusing me of deliberately betraying his trust. I just sat there, not even trying to defend myself. Why bother? He was no idiot. Finally he left, slamming the door behind him, leaving me to understand that he could never forgive me and refused to admit that he was plain terrified by the idea of being a father, with all the responsibilities it entailed. He disappeared into the night and I didn't see him until a few days later when he came back to get his things. It was a very hard day. He gave me no chance to explain or try and make him understand how important the desire for a child had become. The breakup was final, definite and complete.

I was devastated. In the following weeks, I missed a lot of work, mumbling something about a mysterious illness. My general attitude was far from charming... and you have to be charming when you work at a dating agency. My work performance was on the decline, and finally one day my boss overheard me being downright rude to a would-be customer. He fired me on the spot. So now I was not only single but jobless as well. I tried to get a grip on myself and come around to the idea of looking for another job. Time passed — it does have a way of flying by, sometimes — and my situation showed no improvement. The only time I reacted was when my landlord gave me an ultimatum after I told him one too many times that I'd "forgotten" to pay the rent. Finally I pulled myself together, found a job in another dating agency, and got a bit of order back in my life.

But I felt really alone. My breakup was still very recent. However, I had to admit that what I missed most was not so much Jerome, but the part of his anatomy that contained that necessary ingredient for making a baby. I had not put the idea out of my mind, far from it. I wanted that baby more than ever. I even told myself any man would do, as long as he had a good disposition and other qualities I wished to transmit to my child.

153

I started to look more closely at the men I knew, examining them with a critical eye. Nothing of interest there. I had some very nice male friends, but the idea of going to bed with any of them seemed too strange, almost incestuous. What's more, one of them was gay, the other happily married, and the third one too unstable, both financially and emotionally. Next I tried the agency I worked for. "What better place to find the perfect father?" I said to myself, full of enthusiasm. It was simple. All I had to do was search through the files of all available men and determine their "pedigree", at my leisure. Many of these men seemed like good candidates... I'd long since stopped believing that the clientele of dating agencies was solely made up of losers and dropouts!

I got right down to work. Isn't the computer a wonderful research tool? I made a first selection on the basis of a few vague criteria, like age, height and social standing. Did I want someone single or not? A married man would have the advantage of not being around too much... but he also might not be available on the nights I really needed him! My experience with Jerome was enough to convince me that you don't get pregnant on your first try! No, he'd have to be single. I'd just get rid of him after if I had to. I left the age category fairly open so as not to limit my research unnecessarily. Next, height... If I had a boy, I'd want him to be tall and athletic. Hair colour? I chose brown or black. Eye colour? Hazel, why not. I decided not to get into the "special interests" category, preferring to examine each case separately. Finally I pushed the "return" key one last time, and so began my research for the ideal man. The computer pondered for a few moments, then presented me with my first file: fourteen candidates. Fourteen! Fantastic! But my excitement dropped a few notches when I read the data on the screen.

"John, fifty-four, single. Currently unemployed. John is looking for a classy, sexy companion, and is not afraid to broaden his horizons in order to discover the pleasures of life."

I had nothing against broadening my horizons and considered myself fairly sexy. But this John, though six feet tall, was seriously overweight. That was no father for my son, and certainly not for my daughter! I continued reading.

"Stan, twenty-two, marathon runner."

Hmm, this was interesting! A bit young, but that wasn't a problem. Quite the opposite! But as I read on, I saw he was looking for a man in his forties who was as athletic as he was. Too bad! Next...

"Maurice, thirty-six, architect. He likes going for walks in the forest, water sports and nature in general. He's looking for a woman who's available, a non-smoker, for conversation and romance. Overweight and over thirty need not apply."

Again I was discouraged by the photo. Maurice was wearing glasses so thick that it was hard to see what his eyes really looked like. I wanted my child to have perfect vision... And the list went on. Sure, some of the men looked interesting at first view, but there was always some detail that was not quite right. My initial enchantment gradually faded as I read on. Either his teeth were a bit crooked — think of the orthodontist bills! — or he had no hair. A bald man could be very sexy — but not when you could see his nose hairs, even in a computer photo! Another man, Greg, might have suited me, except he had to travel a lot for his work. The lack of availability might prove tricky. Peter lived with four cats, and I couldn't stand those two-faced, unpredictable animals. As for Michael, the dog-trainer, I'd been allergic to every kind of dog since I was little. Then there was that charming doctor, but he specified that he was looking for a woman who could dominate him and make him her slave... definitely not a character trait I wanted my child to inherit! To make a long story short, there was nothing very exciting in this bunch, and I started to get sick of it all, until I came upon something that was decidedly appealing.

"Louis, thirty-nine, contractor. He likes intimate meals and is an excellent cook. His favourite sports are swimming, inline skating and downhill skiing. Louis is looking for a female companion to share these pleasures with, and maybe others too." Judging from the photo he had the physical assets that most appealed to me. Without waiting another instant, I left a message on his voice-mail, hoping he would phone me back quickly.

He phoned me the next day, and our conversation, though brief, was very pleasant. He had a charming sense of humour, and a soft warm voice. As he was talking, I could hear children laughing in the background. I asked him if they were his children.

— No, unfortunately. My sister left them with me for the evening.

We made a date for the next day in a popular café.

I was sitting at a little table in the corner when he appeared. Curly light brown hair, almost shoulder length, and bright, impish hazel eyes, a straight nose with a few pale freckles, sensual lips and perfect teeth. He was splendid!

I got straight to the point. It's my habit to be direct.

— How come you're using a dating agency? You must not

have any trouble meeting pretty women.

— Not as pretty as you! Anyway, I might ask you the same question...

I flashed him my most charming smile as he sat down at the table. We spent several pleasant hours together and went our separate ways with regret, making a date for the following day.

* * *

Over the next few weeks, I had plenty of time to get to know the man behind all these charming assets. Jovial and energetic by nature, he was knowledgeable on all sorts of subjects, which made him a fascinating conversationalist. But conversation, though pleasant and important, was not where he excelled most. Louis was an incredible lover. He had a cosy little house in the Laurentians and took me there as soon as he knew we were attracted to each other. Our first night together was extraordinary, and I remember it fondly to this day.

He made me a delicious meal, serving it in the big living room by a roaring fire he had made in the stone fireplace. The decor was simple but so welcoming! The meal was exquisite, from soup to dessert — especially dessert! All evening we looked into each other's eyes, lingering gazes that hinted at the very pleasant night ahead. He kissed me just before he cleared the table, and came back with a big bowl of strawberries, whipped cream and champagne. He made me dance to soft music in his arms by the fire, undressing me slowly, letting his hazel gaze penetrate deep into my eyes. His eyes were lit with a special glow, full of tenderness. He drew me down onto a bearskin by the hearth, admiring the reflection of the flames on my skin, and slipped strawberries into my mouth one by one, daubing whipped cream with his other hand on my erect nipples, belly and thighs. He licked my skin with avid flicks of his tongue, making swirls in the thick cream.

He seemed to be having a real feast, and told me my skin was exquisite. When the heat of his breath made the cream slide down my thighs, he sighed and tasted the mixture, which he said was sublime. Certainly, the sensation was delectable...

Now naked himself, he slid onto my body, his movements becoming a sort of languorous rubbing. He hovered over me, his pointed sex tickling my face without getting close enough for me to taste it, then my breasts, which I squeezed around him. He gently slid between them, then continued down to my belly, resting a moment at the place my body opened to him. Finally, with a single stroke, he slid inside me and made love to me at first tenderly, then with mounting ardour. My pleasure was intense and I didn't want it to end... I tried to slow his movements, wrapping my legs around his taut waist. I held him still for a moment, trying to guess as I looked deep into his eyes if he appreciated me as much as I did him. What I saw reassured me, the spark in his eyes blazed more brightly than ever. Now I wanted to taste the mixture of his skin and whipped cream. I made him lie down beside me and generously spread the cream over him, taking care to cover every inch of his impatient member, belly and thighs. His taste in my mouth was sweet, delicious. He filled me completely, crushing against my jaw and sliding down to my throat. The cream, now liquid, trailed down my neck to my breasts, which he eagerly started licking.

Kneeling over him, I guided him back to my moist slot,

welcoming him with gratitude and greed. His legs rocked me gently while his hands grabbed my buttocks, lifted me and lowered me down onto his cock like some divine sort of swing. We were a single entity, two parts of the same organism. Louis slipped out of me and plunged his mouth down between my thighs. He tasted me slowly, like a succulent meal, nibbling and sucking with precise, artful movements. I could see my body reflected in the big windows, illuminated by the bright flames. My hair almost completely covered my face, and his head poked out between my spread thighs. I watched him like this for a moment, stroking my quivering breasts, fascinated by this man's head working over the most sensitive part of my body. His tongue lapped at me, he kissed me so much and so well that I came between his lips, my own lips opening in a long shuddering sigh.

I lay down, breasts crushing against the soft fur, letting my lover penetrate me deeply until his sap mingled with mine, and all the other flavours on our burning skin.

Huddling together, we fell asleep by the fire. It was fantastic.

That night, I decided Louis was the ideal man to make me the child I wanted so badly. There was only one cloud on the horizon. I was struggling with a serious dilemma. I could tell him my intentions, and risk seeing him run away as fast as he could. Or I could just not say anything, let nature do its work, and decide later, depending on how our relationship was going. I spent a few days thinking about it and finally decided on the second option. I wouldn't say anything but just enjoy making love, without taking precautions... you never knew! Once again I started calculating what dates would best serve my purposes. The next month, I took a break from my lover a few days before I ovulated.

Of course I missed him, but I wanted this wait to make our desire (and his sperm) as strong as possible. I had assured him that I was planning a dynamite weekend for us, and phoned him Friday afternoon to make a date, but just got the answering machine.

"Hi, you've reached Louis and Dan. Leave a message and we'll get back to you as soon as we can!"

"Louis, it's Caroline. I hope you're not busy tonight. I really want to see you, as soon as possible. I'm at home, and I'm not moving... except to take off my clothes... BEEP!"

Dan... Louis had barely mentioned this brother with whom he shared his apartment in the city. I'd never met him, the times I'd stayed at Louis' place instead of the house in the Laurentians. I was getting a bit curious, but figured I'd meet him sooner or later.

I took a bath and lay happily soaking for almost an hour, then slathered myself with fragrant body lotion. I took extra special care with my appearance, choosing a pretty little silk negligee and a long dressing gown. Time passed, and Louis hadn't shown any sign of life. But that was okay! He wouldn't phone unless he really couldn't come over, after that very clear message I'd left him!

I picked up a book I'd started the day before. About half an hour later, I heard a knock at the door. I turned off the lamp, creating the desired atmosphere in the room, and went to open the door, light of heart. He was standing there with a beautiful bouquet of flowers. He pulled me against him and kissed me passionately. I was flattered to see that he'd been in such a hurry, he hadn't even stopped to shave! His cheek was rough against my skin. I drew him inside and without even giving him time to take off his coat, started undressing before him.

— Will you greet me like that every time I come over?

— If you want...

— Promise me! Every time...

— I promise.

His wish confirmed, he stripped off his clothes, drew me onto the sofa and plunged his mouth between my naked thighs. He licked me until I was streaming, and I begged him to make love to me hard and fast. I was gasping with pleasure, but wanted to delay my orgasm until I could finally feel him inside me. He had to come a lot, as deeply as possible inside me. He absolutely had to...

He finally answered my prayers, taking hold of me roughly then turning me around and penetrating me, grinding at my open sex, plunging deep inside me with almost brutal thrusts. I sensed he was close to the blessed moment when he would come inside my body. I tried to follow his rhythm, his pleasure. Just as he was about to explode, the phone rang. I was about to tell him I wasn't going to answer, but didn't get the chance. Startled by the ill-timed ringing, he pulled out for a second, and just at that moment came with a powerful gush on my buttocks and lower back. I made a supreme effort not to show my disappointment. No, no, I wasn't disappointed by his performance, far from it! But today was one of those "potentially fertile" days, and he had wasted precious millilitres of fluid on my behind rather than inside me, where it should have gone! Well, too bad. I'd try again later.

Unfortunately, Louis had to go back home that night because he was waiting for an overseas phonecall. I sadly watched him get ready to leave, and asked him to come back the next day, emphasizing that he would get the same sort of welcome. I watched him leave with regret, promising

myself that I would have my way with him the next day...
and not just once!

* * *

The next day I was irritable and nervous. I realized that
my lack of honesty with Louis was bothering me. But at the
same time, I didn't want to spoil my chances of making my
secret dream come true! It was as if I had an intuition that
the next time it would work, that this would be the month
when the long-awaited event would finally occur. I would
see his reaction afterwards. If I had to, I was ready to take
sole responsibility for my actions.

The minutes ticked by, the afternoon seemed to last forever. Would he come back that evening? He had to come,
and this time come in the right place! To make him understand how much I wanted to see him, and make sure he
would visit, I phoned him late in the afternoon. Again I got
the answering machine, which annoyed me even more. I
froze, not knowing what kind of message to leave... then
hung up. The message couldn't be too intimate, in case his
brother heard it first. But it also had to clearly convey how
much I desired him. Well, too bad for the brother! Let him
think what he liked! I dialed the number again, patiently
waited for the message to come to an end, and got right to
the point.

"Louis... I miss you! I absolutely have to see you tonight!
If you only knew how impatient I am to see you! I'll greet
you at the door, the way I promised, the way you like it.
Don't be long... BEEP!"

"When he hears that," I thought, "how could he not
come straight over?"

The wait was even shorter than I thought. I barely had

time to take a quick after-work shower and change clothes before I heard someone banging at the door. I ran to open it, ready to strip off my clothes as soon as he got in. He was so handsome! His hazel eyes, with what seemed like an unusual glow, went right through me, sweeping up and down my body, full of mischief and desire. He undressed me with his eyes, and my breathing quickened, I was almost breathless before his appraising stare that was impudent and flattering both at once. I pulled him to me without waiting another second. His dizzying cologne made me pull back, and then it was my turn to be impudent. I let the light garment slide off my shivering shoulders. Louis picked me up a little roughly and let me fall back on the couch. He tore off his jacket, shirt and pants with frantic gestures and bent over me.

— I didn't dare hope you'd get here so fast...

— When I got your message, nothing could've held me back. But I can't stay long... you won't be mad if I leave right after?

— Not if you do what I've been wanting you to do since you left...

To show me he understood, he kneeled down between my legs and kissed my already damp lips. Then his hand took over and he caressed me roughly, almost chafing the delicate flesh — but what a sweet pain! Spreading the folds of my inflamed sex, he became more insistent, inserting a finger, then another, between the velvety walls deep inside my body. The sensation of his finger moving in and out was sharpened by a firm pressure on just the right spot, which threatened to make me come at any second. He'd never turned me on this much before! Lifting my hips between his powerful hands, he pushed his cock into me, it felt huge, thrusting into the depths of my body while continuing the circular movement of his finger on my sex, which was pulsing to the rhythm of my heart. I was about to come fast and furious when he pulled me up and made me kneel over with elbows on the back of the sofa. He pulled my hips back so my spread buttocks were displayed before him. He continued stroking me, letting his hand slide in front then between my trembling lips that he spread before thrusting again, forcing his member in to the hilt. I cried out with pleasure, I couldn't hold myself back any more, and came with such intensity I was almost out of my mind.

My surrender only increased Louis' ardour. Seizing my pelvis with both hands, he pounded into me hard until I was sure I was going to explode. I welcomed his onslaught with greedy lust, my body threatening once more to succumb. I came again, a few seconds before Louis climaxed in one last wild jolt, filling me to the brim, just as I had hoped — and I knew how important this detail was. I felt the weight of his body gently crushing me. I pulled him against me, pushing back against his warm belly and melting into a huge sense of well-being. My entire body was still shaking with pleasure, but my head was heavy with a wonderful fatigue. I didn't make the slightest move to stop him when he got up, kissed my hair, and told me he absolutely had to go. He quickly pulled on his clothes, kissed me again, and disappeared.

I remained this way for some time, not wanting to disturb the sweet torpor that filled my body. Finally, my legs trembling, I pulled myself to my feet and picked up my clothes, shivering with pleasure at the thought of a warm bath. At that moment, I spotted something lying on the floor, almost hidden under the sofa. I bent over to pick it up and saw it was a wallet — Louis' wallet, I supposed. I was about to put it on the little table by the door when I saw that some cards and papers had fallen out. I leaned over to look at them and something caught my attention: a health-care card. The photo on the card wasn't very flattering, those photos never are. But it wasn't this detail that made me jump... Under the photo, instead of the LOUIS BENSON that I'd expected to see, I read DAN BENSON. His brother? His twin brother?! I fell back heavily onto the sofa, dazed. Louis had never mentioned a *twin* brother! A brother, yes... I thought of the message on the answering machine: "Hi, you've reached Louis and Dan..."

"No!... That was Louis who just left", I told myself. "I would have known if it wasn't him!"

But would I have, really?

The phone interrupted my thoughts. I answered almost in a whisper, trying not to betray how upset I was. It was Louis, he'd been delayed downtown and had just picked up his messages... Could he come over later? I told him I'd be waiting, and swallowed the lump in my throat, thinking of the enormity of the situation. More upset than ever, I started running a bath, which would no doubt do me a world of good, stubbornly refusing to think until I was submerged in hot water and fragrant bubbles.

Once in the bath, I allowed myself a few moments' reflection. Strangely enough, I had no feelings of embarrassment, shame or betrayal about what had just happened. If Dan was really Louis' twin brother, and if it was he who had just made love to me so well, what was the problem? Louis would never have to find out! The only problem lay in the fact that I was apparently incapable of telling them apart. But the more I thought about it, the more I told myself how lucky I was! Two for the price of one! What woman would dream of complaining? And if Louis ever learned what happened, how would he react? Had this ever happened with another woman? Was this some kind of game the brothers indulged in for kicks? If that was the case, the situation became more disturbing. However, instinct told me that Louis knew nothing about it — and it wasn't going to be me who let the cat out of the bag! I would simply have to find some way of telling them apart. Louis was the one I liked best. Maybe if I'd met Dan first, I'd have gotten hooked on him instead! But the most important thing was not to do anything to hurt Louis. If I played my cards right, everything would work out fine. When he came over later, I wouldn't say anything about his brother's surprise visit. Not a word! But how to tell if it was really him? I would ask him precise questions on things we'd done together. But what if it wasn't the first time this kind of substitution had happened? Oh, it was all too complicated! Still, one twin or the other, it was all the same to me, as long as I achieved my goal... and this evening, I would have an even better chance of doing so!

The image of the two brothers came back into my mind, bringing with it a very pleasant fantasy. I let myself slide deeper into the tub, and explored this new vision. I was lying on my bed, longing for Louis. The daydream turned into the present moment. He arrived, got slowly undressed and kissed me. His naked body on mine made me shiver. Almost totally passive, I let his lips brush tenderly over my throat, my breasts, belly and legs. His tongue teased the opening of my willing pussy, and it was then that Dan appeared. He got undressed too, kissed my mouth, while Louis multiplied his caresses below, way down. Hands — I don't know whose — kneaded my breasts, lips sucked them with ardour, while other hands and lips skillfully worked between my open thighs. A member forced my mouth open, pushed its way back towards my throat, while another entered me brutally, spreading my thighs even wider apart. The rhythm of the two members was the same, but alternating. Then one of the men fell onto his back — I don't know which one — and I went to his hard cock and took it into my greedy mouth while another man shoved into me from behind. Who was it, Louis or Dan? Had they changed roles, or was it the same man I'd sucked into my body so passionately before? I didn't care. The bodies started moving again and I was on my knees, on the floor, one erect member in front of my face, another thrusting into my body. Hands seized my breasts, others my hair, my buttocks... how many hands? How many majestic hard cocks were doing me this honour? Finally the man behind me let himself come, followed seconds later by his brother, imprisoned between my lips. The liquid gushed over my mouth, throat, sex, thighs... And I came, floating in my now lukewarm bath, my hands buried between my legs.

* * *

When Louis arrived later that evening, I waited a little before starting with the questions I wanted so badly to ask. I was content to repeat the same movements as a few hours before, letting my skimpy garment slide to the floor, waiting for him to drag me onto the sofa. But he chose the bedroom instead. I had a hard time concentrating on the present, because my new fantasy kept coming back to haunt me. Would I one day have the experience that made me wet with desire just thinking about it? Who knows, maybe, if I played my cards right... My ardour was genuine beneath Louis' caresses (but was it really him?), and I came once again. Louis took me from the front, from behind, on my knees, standing, delaying his own orgasm to give me pleasure as long as possible. But I was exhausted... I tried to hurry him up, though taking full advantage of the delicious sensations he was giving me, and finally he came inside me. I happily collapsed into his arms.

I waited a few moments before starting my interrogation. His breathing was getting slower and deeper, I didn't want him to go to sleep so fired away with my first question.

— Are you ever going to introduce me to your brother?

— My brother? Why?

— I've left two pretty suggestive messages on your answering machine. I'd like to meet him soon, or he might get the wrong idea about me...

— Well, maybe some day...

— How old is he?

— Just a few minutes older than me. We're twins.

— Really? Do you look alike?

— We're identical, except for a few minor details.

— Now I really want to meet him!

I adopted a teasing tone, in case it was a touchy subject. But he just laughed and asked me:

— Why, aren't I enough for you?

— Oh, yes, I think you'll do! But tell me, what are these "minor details"? Hair, moustache — something like that?

— No... As a matter of fact, we've always liked to have the same haircut and look as much alike as possible. But his eyes are a bit lighter than mine, and he has a scar on his forehead, just at the hairline. He got it a few years ago.

— You're kidding... those are the only differences?

— People who know us well say we don't have the same look. They say he looks a bit tougher than me. But I can't tell if it's true or not. As for meeting him, maybe you will. But my past girlfriends were disturbed by how much we looked alike... And besides, I found you first!

I changed the subject, convinced he had no idea I knew his brother already. From now on, I would just have to look at their foreheads!

* * *

I saw Louis several times in the next week, making sure it was him when he arrived at my place. It had become a sort of joke, the way he brushed his hair off his forehead before he came in so I could see if there was a scar. I didn't see Dan again, but simply returned his wallet anonymously by mail. Louis had to go out of town on business, so we spent a few wonderful days at his house in the Laurentians, basking in the sweet odour of burning wood and watching the snow fall outside. I didn't ask again about his brother, waiting for Louis to bring him up first.

However, the image of two identical men making love to me kept coming back to haunt me. The fantasy got stronger and stronger, until I couldn't spend an evening with Louis without expecting to see his lookalike appear at any minute. I was so obsessed with the idea that it took me three days to realize that my period was late. Was it possible — at long last? I was overjoyed that I'd finally succeeded in giving myself the gift I'd been dreaming about for so long. Still, I waited a few more days before getting confirmation.

When I was almost ten days overdue, I went to the drug-store to get a pregnancy test kit. I feverishly read the in-structions and got down to my task. Two minutes later, the verdict came in loud and clear: I was pregnant! I dove to the phone and made the first possible appointment with my doctor. He confirmed the news a few days later. I was ecstatic! Oh, sure, there'd be a bit of nausea from time to time, but that was nothing compared to the joy I felt. Louis was coming back soon, and I still didn't know how to tell him. Obviously I couldn't hide it forever... And I'd decided to tell him that he was free to get involved with the child or not, as he wished. If he wanted to play father, so much the better, but I wouldn't force him.

The main thing that worried me was that the child's father could very well be Dan... that, I could not tell Louis. How could I? Nonetheless I was dying of curiosity. Was it Louis or Dan? Obviously I'd never know.

I went to get Louis at the airport. When he saw me, he realized there was something different about me. My resolution to wait before telling him the happy news dissolved in a flash. I told him he was going to be a father in a few months. Before he could react, I insisted I had no expectations, that he was free to act as he wished. His face broke into a huge smile and he assured me he would be there as much as I wanted, that he would spend as much time as he could with the child. Everything was turning out for the best!

But this was not the end of it. My infidelity with his brother, though totally unpremeditated, worried me to no end. I felt I had done something terribly wrong, but at the same time realized this "wrong" may have made me pregnant at last. When Louis finally decided to introduce me to his brother, and his brother learned the news, would he realize it might possibly involve him? Probably not. But I still couldn't help asking myself what consequences his visit might have had...

In the following weeks, I was in a state of constant anxiety. Louis put my nervousness down to my pregnancy, and I did nothing to let him know what the real reason was. The day of my ultrasound, I was convinced I'd get a sign as to who the real father was. But what sign could there be? I didn't have the slightest idea, and I knew I was being totally irrational. Still, I was convinced. Maybe I'd see something during the test that would resolve the mystery. Or maybe I'd know by intuition, at the moment I least expected, who the father was.

The waiting room was packed. I was wringing my hands with nervousness, thinking of names I liked, boys' and girls' names all mixed together. When my turn came, I was a wreck, barely able to get myself to the room where I'd been told to go. I lay down on the table, waiting for the technician to smear gel on my stomach then apply the instrument that would allow me to see my baby. I looked at the device anxiously. The technican asked me, before she began, if I wanted to know the sex of my child. I nodded vigorously, and she went ahead. A big smile appeared on her face.

"Ms. Lainey," she said, "you've got twins! A little boy... and a little girl! Congratulations!"

MEMBRE DU GROUPE SCABRINI

Québec, Canada
2000